Christmas of Joy
A River Falls Christmas Romance

Valerie M. Bodden

River Falls Series

Pieces of Forever
Songs of Home
Memories of the Heart
Whispers of Truth
Promises of Mercy
Hearts of Hope

River Falls Christmas Romances

Christmas of Joy

Hope Springs Series

Not Until Forever
Not Until This Moment
Not Until You
Not Until Us
Not Until Christmas Morning
Not Until This Day
Not Until Someday
Not Until Now
Not Until Then
Not Until The End

Love on Sanctuary Shores

Trusting His Promise

A Gift for You

Members of my Reader's Club get a FREE book, available exclusively to my subscribers. When you sign up, you'll also be the first to know about new releases, book deals, and giveaways.
Visit www.valeriembodden.com/freebook to join!

River Falls Character Map

If you love the whole Calvano family but need a refresher of who's who, what they do, and which book belongs to each, check out the handy character map at www.valeriembodden.com/rfcharacters

The joy of the Lord is your strength.

Nehemiah 8:10

Chapter 1

"You'll be my maid of honor, of course."

"I will?" Madison choked around her sip of water, nearly dropping the crystal goblet Mom insisted on using even for a simple family brunch.

Melanie tsked. "Well, you're the only sister I have."

"I'm honored." Madison rolled her eyes, but Mel waved off her comment as if it were nothing more substantial than the smoke from the candles in the middle of the table.

"So anyway," Mel continued. "The wedding is December 16."

"December 16?" Madison set her goblet down hard, earning a reproving look from Mom. "That's only like five weeks away." She shouldn't be surprised. Her sister had always been a take-action kind of person. She knew what she wanted, and she went for it without hesitation. Unlike Madison.

Melanie stabbed her fork into a slice of strawberry. "We're just lucky we were both able to get off. The hospital wasn't thrilled with losing two residents at once. So anyway—" She turned to Mom. "We were thinking we could have the engagement party on Saturday and then—"

"I can't on Saturday," Madison interrupted.

Mom, Dad, and Mel all turned to her, and Madison fully expected to get scolded by one or all of them for interrupting.

Mom's thin eyebrows drew together. "I'm sure you can cancel whatever plans you had. This is your sister's engagement party we're talking about."

"Yes. That I just learned about three minutes ago." Madison clutched the napkin in her lap. "I committed to running a fundraiser for Dr. Calvano months ago."

"I'm sure he can find someone else to do it." Mom turned back to Mel. "We'll have it here. What should we serve? How about those—"

"No." Madison interrupted again.

"No, what?" Mom spoke way too deliberately.

"No, he can't find someone else to do it. This is my project. My responsibility." She'd dedicated every free moment for months to planning it.

At the other end of the table, Dad covered a muted cough. "That's refreshing to hear."

Madison braced herself. Was he really going to bring up—

"Unlike the time I asked you to organize the company Christmas party."

Yes. Yes, he was going to bring it up.

"I was nineteen, Dad. I didn't know what I was doing."

"Mmm." The only thing more infuriating than Dad's tone was the look of disappointment he wore, as if it had just happened yesterday, rather than eight years ago.

"Well, what time does your fundraiser get done?" Mel asked, shooting Madison a pitying look she didn't need.

"Eleven o'clock."

"Eleven a.m.?" Mel clarified.

"Yes. Of course."

"Well, then there's no problem." Mel smiled as if she'd just single-handedly brought about world peace. "The party will be at night. Seven o'clock?" She turned to Mom, and Madison knew her input was dismissed.

She tried not to be hurt that no one had even asked about her fundraiser. Mel had just announced she was getting married; a fundraiser was nothing compared to that.

Madison swirled her fork through the syrup that remained on her plate after the French toast was gone. Somehow Mom managed to discuss wedding plans with Mel and shoot Madison a "cease and desist" look at the same time.

Madison set her fork down and folded her hands in her lap, listening as Mom and Melanie planned the party down to the very last detail, making quick decisions and placing orders right there at the table. She thought about asking whether Brad might want to have some say in things but decided it was best to hold her tongue. Finally, Dad set down his napkin and pushed back his chair. The universal signal that the meal was over.

Madison heaved a sigh and jumped up from the table.

"Thanks for brunch." She pecked her Mom on the cheek. "I have to run, but I guess I'll see you at the party next weekend."

"Where are you off to in such a hurry?" Mom eyed her, as if she might be headed out to loot in the streets.

"Oh, I have a bunch of housework to catch up on." She waved off the question. She wasn't ready to tell them the truth quite yet.

Mom frowned. "You work part-time and still can't keep up with your housework?"

Madison bit her tongue. Easy for Mom to say, when she had a maid come in three times a week. But if Madison pointed that out, Mom would only counter with how much more demanding her own job as vice president of Dad's mortgage company was.

"Are you keeping up with your bills?" Dad called from the leather couch he'd settled on.

"Yes, Dad." Madison tried not to sound impatient. Taking this job with Dr. Calvano was supposed to show her family that she was more than a flighty little girl with no purpose. That she was a woman of substance.

"And have you moved out of that tiny apartment yet?" Mom asked.

Madison pressed her lips together. Did Mom really think she'd moved and not told them? "I still live there, Mom." Somehow she managed to keep her voice pleasant. And not point out that Mel's apartment was just as small.

Anyway, Madison liked her place. It might not be luxurious, like this house, but it was quiet and cozy. And it was hers. Paid for with her own hard-earned money.

She moved to the front closet and pulled out the thigh-length gray wool coat Mom had given her for Christmas last year. She made sure her sweater sleeves were all the way down before pulling it on, so she wouldn't have itchy skin the rest of the day.

"Oh wait. I almost forgot to give you this." Mel rushed at her, holding out what looked like a business card.

Madison took it, her eyes scanning the logo. L&M Auto. "What's this?"

"Luke's card."

"Luke?" Madison's mouth went dry as her eyes fell on his name near the bottom of the card. "Why would I need Luke's card?"

Melanie laughed. "Well, Luke is Bradley's only brother, so . . ." She waved a hand through the air, as if waiting for Madison to catch on.

"So Luke is the best man?" Madison's hand had gone numb, holding the card in front of her face. The address was right here in River Falls. But that couldn't be right.

"I thought he moved to Georgia." And had gotten married, if she'd heard correctly.

"Yes." Melanie dragged out the word as if Madison were slow. "But he moved back to Tennessee now."

"When?" Madison demanded. She was usually up on the comings and goings in River Falls—everyone was. But she hadn't heard a whisper of Luke's return. "Why didn't you say anything?"

Mel gave her an odd look. "A month or two ago. And I don't think I've seen you since then. I've only seen *him* once, at dinner with Brad's parents."

Madison sucked her cheeks against her teeth so she wouldn't ask how he'd looked. How he was doing. If he'd asked about her.

"Oooh." Mel gave her a teasing look. "I forgot you used to have a thing for him."

"I did not." Madison tugged at the sleeves of her jacket. It was only slightly less comfortable than this conversation.

"Yes, you did." Mel laughed, pointing at her. "The way you used to follow him around everywhere."

Madison ducked her head, wishing she could deny it. But she'd been a silly schoolgirl then, when their families had summered together at Hilton Head and gone to each other's houses for Christmas.

"What does he do now?" Mom asked, raising an eyebrow at Madison.

"He's a mechanic," Mel answered, and Madison glanced at the card.

According to this, he wasn't just a mechanic. He was co-owner of the business.

Good for him.

"It's not going to be a problem, is it?" Mel asked.

"That he's a mechanic?" Madison wrinkled her nose. Of course it wouldn't—

"No. That you used to have a crush on him, silly." Mel shoved her shoulder.

"No. I mean, I didn't. I mean, a problem for what?" Madison blew a breath upward in desperate hope of cooling her face. She was going to melt right into the floor if she had to stand here much longer.

"Planning our Jack and Jill party."

"Your what?" Madison stared at her sister. She wanted a nursery rhyme party?

"You know. Instead of bachelor and bachelorette parties. We want to do something together. Something classy. Not cheesy. Preferably in the next week or two, so there will be enough time before the wedding."

"The next week or two?" Madison mentally scrolled through the pile of things she had going on in the next two weeks, including the fundraiser, plus multiple exams to study for and a major paper to write.

She swallowed. "I can make that happen."

"Good. And it's not like you have to do it all yourself. You and Luke can plan it together." Mel winked. "Make sure you give him a call."

"Yeah." Madison's voice had become an odd croak. "I will."

She made her escape out the door, pausing outside her car to gaze down the mountainside toward River Falls, nestled below.

Luke was really back.

The first boy she'd ever kissed. The one who had crushed her teenage heart.

Chapter 2

"There," Luke murmured with a final torque of the wrench. "Let's see what you think of that, Miss Sally." He pulled his head out from the hood of the 1969 Mustang Boss and moved toward the driver's seat. This car had been in sad shape when he'd gotten it. Sad enough that his partner Mitch had only laughed and shaken his head when he'd seen it. But Luke knew the old girl still had life in her. All she needed was a little love to bring it out.

He snorted as he dropped into the seat. If the car needed love, she was out of luck. Fortunately, what she really needed was mechanical prowess. And that he had plenty of. Sally here would appreciate that, even if his ex-wife hadn't.

He grunted. Three years later, and he still wasn't used to that little prefix. How were two small letters supposed to represent everything that he'd lost when his marriage fell apart?

He jabbed the key into the ignition and turned. The engine coughed once, twice, then fell silent.

Luke heaved a sigh and patted the steering wheel. "It's all right, girl. I'm not giving up on you yet."

He glanced across the garage to the 1977 Camaro he and Mitch had pulled apart. That one they were going to resell—hopefully for a tidy profit. Maybe enough to put some new lifts in this old garage. But this one—he patted the roof as he got out of the car—this one was just for him.

The shop phone rang from the other side of the garage, and Luke sighed, wiping his hands on his coveralls as he jogged toward it. If it were up to him, he'd never answer the phone. But Mitch seemed to think that wasn't a good way to run a business.

Mitch's call a couple months ago, inviting him to come back to Tennessee and open their own shop, had caught Luke completely by surprise. The two had been friends as kids—and had even restored an old F-150 together back in the day—but they'd lost touch when Luke moved to Georgia after high school to work in his uncle's shop. But Mitch had tracked him down through social media—and Luke had been more than ready for a change. And now here he was—co-owner of a business. A small, just-getting-off-the-ground business, but a business just the same.

And that meant answering the phone.

He grabbed it off the workbench and pulled it to his ear.

"Hello?"

There was no response.

"Hello?" he repeated.

Nothing.

Luke growled. He'd missed the call. That figured.

He pulled the phone away from his ear and was about to hang up when he thought he heard a faint "hello" through the speaker.

He lifted it to his ear again. "Hello? Can I help you?"

"Luke?"

Luke stilled. The voice was strangely familiar.

"Madicake?"

The huff confirmed it. "You know I hate that name."

Luke grinned. "I know."

"Stop grinning."

"I'm not grinning."

"Yes you are. I can hear it."

"Last I checked, you couldn't hear a grin. Now, how can I help you?" He tapped speaker and set the phone on the workbench, rummaging through a half-organized pile of tools. There had to be an air ratchet in here somewhere.

"You haven't changed at all, have you?"

Luke snorted but shook his head. If only she knew how much he'd changed. The last time he saw her, he was eighteen. And now he was thirty. Married. And divorced. But somehow, hearing her voice seemed to erase all of that. "Nope. I'm still the same charming, good-looking—"

"Stop it." Madison huffed again, and Luke almost made another swaggering comment just for fun, but he held back.

"So what do you think we should do?" Madison asked.

"I'm sorry?" Not that he'd necessarily be opposed to doing something with her, but it seemed rather presumptuous to assume the yes without asking.

Besides, he *wouldn't* say yes. He couldn't. He was done with dating. Done with marrying. Done with women. Period.

It's Madison, his heart argued.

Right. Which only made her three times more dangerous than the average woman.

"For Melanie and Brad's Jack and Jill thingy," Madison clarified. "I hear you're the best man. And I'm the maid of honor, so . . ."

"You are?" When Brad had asked him to be the best man, Luke hadn't even thought to ask who Melanie had chosen as maid of honor. But it made sense that it would be her only sister.

"Yes. Is that a problem?" Madison sounded suddenly defensive, and Luke chuckled at the fire in her voice.

"No problem at all," he drawled. "As long as it's not a problem for you."

"Why would it be a problem for me?"

"I guess it wouldn't be." Luke caught a glimpse of the air ratchet half buried under a pile of socket wrenches. He reached for it, knocking down a metallic box of drill bits in the process. It hit the floor with a clang and opened, spilling its contents far and wide. Luke groaned.

"What was that?"

"What was what?" Luke bent to start picking up the bits.

"That sound."

"What sound?"

Madison huffed again, and Luke chuckled harder.

"Never mind. Look, did Brad tell you that they want to do some kind of joint party thing? But I don't think they really want a party. Something 'classy,' Mel said." He could hear the air quotes in Madison's voice, and he snickered.

"What?"

"Nothing. You just don't seem to appreciate their idea."

"It's fine. I just have a lot to do, without adding this on top. Anyway, I just wanted to let you know that I'll figure something out, so you don't have to worry about it."

Luke dropped the drill bits onto the workbench. "What do you mean I don't have to worry about it?"

"All you have to do is show up. And make sure the rest of the guys show up too. Can you handle that?"

Luke snorted. "Good to know you haven't changed either."

"What?" She sounded genuinely confused.

"Brad is my brother, you know. I'm not just going to sit back and let you do everything. Next thing you know, you'll be making reservations for all of us at some tea room."

Madison's laugh was unexpected—and it drew an unexpected laugh from him too. It came out kind of rusty, as if it'd been too long since he'd used that sound. Her laugh, on the other hand, sounded well-practiced and warm.

"And where do you think we're going to find a tea room in River Falls?" she asked.

"I don't know. I guess you'll just have to open one."

"Yeah, I'll get right on that." Sarcasm dripped from her words, and Luke ate it up. He'd forgotten how fun it was to verbally spar with her.

"Whatever we're going to do, it has to be in the next week or two," Madison continued. "So if you want to help, we have to figure this out fast. Do you want to do it over the phone or—uh—meet, or what?" She sounded suddenly uncertain, and he could imagine her tucking a piece of hair behind her ear, the way she had right before he'd kissed her that time.

"Let's meet." His answer was out before he had time to think about it.

"Uh. Okay." Madison clearly hadn't expected that answer, and Luke smiled to himself. He wasn't sure why keeping her off balance was so fun, but it was. It always had been.

"How about tomorrow?" she asked, still sounding flustered. "I get done with work at five, so maybe quarter after?"

"5:15 works. Daisy's?"

"Sure. See you then." She hung up, and Luke stood grinning at the phone.

Stop it, he scolded himself, trying to reshape his mouth into a frown.

She'd already made it clear years ago that he wasn't her type.

But that didn't mean it wouldn't be nice to see her. For old times' sake.

Chapter 3

Madison tapped on the door to Joseph's office. "Mr. Gray just called and said Poppy ate a whole container of chocolate frosting. I told him to watch her for signs of vomiting or diarrhea. Just a heads-up in case he calls the answering service."

"Again." Joseph rolled his eyes. "Apparently there is no way to get it through that man's head that he can't leave food on the table. Or he has to train his dog not to pull it down. Are you heading out?"

Madison nodded. "Unless you need me to stay? I can." She held her breath. *Please, please, please.*

"And get you out of your date?" Joseph laughed. "Not on your life."

"It's not a date. It's a meeting." Madison crossed her arms. "And you're a terrible boss, do you know that?"

"Yes, I do. Now go, or you'll be late."

She rolled her eyes. "It's literally five blocks from here."

"Yeah. But there could be traffic. You know how River Falls gets at rush hour."

They both laughed, and Madison turned and marched back to her desk, forcing herself to put on her coat, pick up her purse, and head out the door.

A cold wind tugged at her hair, and she snuggled deeper into her coat, tucking her hands into her pockets. The chill urged her feet into a speed walk despite the fact that she'd rather crawl to this meeting. A warm glow of light spilled out the windows of the quaint shops she passed—Henderson's Art Gallery, the Sweet Boutique, the Book Den—many of which were already festooned with Christmas lights. If not for the cold, Madison would linger to admire them.

Instead, too soon, she was opening the door at Daisy's and stepping inside. A wild surge went through her middle as she scanned the cozy pie shop in search of Luke. But the only customers were an older couple and a young mother with her toddler son, who seemed to be throwing some sort of tantrum.

Madison pulled out her phone and checked the time.

5:15, on the dot.

She supposed she could cut him some slack, given that she'd just gotten here as well.

Now what? Should she order some pie? Stand here and wait for him? Take a seat?

She shook her head at herself. It didn't matter what she did. It wasn't like this was a date.

She moved to the register and ordered a piece of cherry pie and a chai tea. By the time it was ready, Luke still hadn't arrived, so she took a seat by the window overlooking the riverwalk that ran behind the shop. Only a few people braved the chill tonight, most walking as quickly as she had, their faces buried in their coats.

Madison watched them as she ate her pie and sipped at her tea.

When her mug was almost empty, she checked the time again. 5:30.

Okay, now she was officially annoyed. He could have at least called and said he'd be late. Did he think she didn't have a life? Didn't have things she needed to do?

She pictured her radiology textbook sitting at home on the kitchen table. She should have brought it along.

She'd give him five more minutes, and then she was out of here. She'd plan everything herself, just like she'd wanted to in the first place.

Suddenly, she found herself feeling hopeful.

She ran a finger back and forth over her lip, watching the clock on her phone. It was moving too slowly.

Occasionally, she darted a glance toward the door, holding her breath every time. One more minute, and she'd be home free.

She started a countdown in her head. Fifty-nine. Fifty-eight. Fifty-seven.

She kept going, eyes locked on the door now.

Thirty-two. Thirty-one. Thirty.

A set of headlights swung into the parking lot and she held her breath, speeding up her count.

Twenty-nine-twenty-eight-twenty-seven.

She'd gotten to ten when the door opened. A woman walked in, and Madison let out a breath.

Nine-eight-seven.

Why wasn't the door closing?

Six. Five.

Two children scooted through.

Four. Three. Two.

Luke.

Madison's breath left her in a rush.

How had he sneaked in here at literally the last second? Was he with the woman and children?

But as the woman and children approached the counter, Luke hung back. His head swiveled, as if he were looking for someone.

Her, she realized with a start. He was looking for her. But he was looking in the wrong direction.

Should she call out to him? Or—

His head turned in her direction, and she found her hand raising, like she was some sort of princess in a parade. She shoved it back into her lap.

But Luke had seen, and he was marching toward her, not exactly smiling but not frowning either.

"Hey." He stopped in front of her table. "Sorry I'm—"

"You're late," she cut him off.

"Yeah." He pulled off the stocking cap that covered his head, revealing the same thick, dark hair she remembered. "That's why I was apologizing."

She nodded curtly.

"I hope you haven't been waiting long." Luke pulled off his jacket to reveal a slightly rumpled button down shirt.

Madison swallowed back her surprise. She'd been expecting the same grease-stained t-shirts he used to live in.

"I figured you'd appreciate if I showered before I came, especially since I had a little mishap and got covered in oil today." His smile was boyish and self-deprecating and it made Madison's lips lift in spite of herself.

Her eyes went to his hands, which still bore traces of oil and hard work.

"I do appreciate it." She gestured at her empty plate. "Do you want some pie? I came right from work and was starving, so I already had a piece."

Luke's eyes went from her plate to her mouth, and he grinned. "Cherry?"

She startled. "You remembered?"

He laughed, shaking his head. "That, and you have some on your face. Right here."

Before she could react, he swept her napkin off the table and swiped it gently over the edge of her lips. A tingle went through them and transformed into a shiver as it traveled down her back.

She wrapped her arms around herself as he strode toward the counter. Halfway there, he turned around, and she averted her eyes so he wouldn't realize she'd been watching.

"You want anything?" he called back to her.

She strained for a casual expression. "I'm good."

He saluted and disappeared around the corner, and Madison let out a slow stream of air. But it wasn't enough to slow her heart rate. She lifted a hand to her lips. They still tingled.

Oh, she was being ridiculous. Sure, she may have had a crush on Luke once upon a time. And sure, he may have been her first kiss. But he'd made it clear afterward that he thought of her as nothing more than a silly little girl.

Well, maybe she had been. Then.

But she wasn't anymore.

She grabbed the napkin off the table and strode to the garbage can to throw it away.

Luke had to keep reminding himself to focus on his pie. Not on the way the soft light played with Madison's honey hair. Or the way her hands clutched the mug of tea he'd gotten her when he'd ordered his pie. Or the way she rubbed a finger absently over her lips from time to time.

He didn't know what he'd been thinking before, wiping the pie filling from those lips.

It had just been . . . instinct.

He nearly snorted at himself. The same instinct that had led him to kiss her that Christmas?

"So." He stabbed at a large bite of pie. "You said you came right from work. What do you do?"

"I'm the office assistant at River Falls Veterinary."

"Oh." He felt his eyebrows go up. "That's good."

Madison set her mug of tea down. "Why do you say it like that?"

"Like what?"

"Like *that*. Like you're surprised."

He shrugged, shoving another bite of pie into his mouth to buy some time. "I guess I *am* surprised," he finally said. "I just never pictured you working with animals." Or working at all, if he was being honest.

Madison frowned at him. "Well, I do. In fact, I'm—" She pushed her hair off her forehead. "You know what, let's just make our plans. I have a lot to do yet tonight."

"Sure." He had plenty of other things to do yet tonight too. There was a half-read book sitting on his coffee table, just waiting for him, thank you very much. "So, I was thinking, what if we went bowling?"

Madison wrinkled her nose.

"Oh, I'm sorry, is bowling beneath you?" He didn't mean to say it with quite so much snark, but really, sometimes she was such a snob.

"No," Madison bit out. "I like to bowl. But my sister does not. And since this is her party, maybe we should do something she would like."

"All right, then. What does your sister like?"

Madison blinked at him. "Well. Um . . ." She closed her eyes and rubbed at her temple.

Luke laughed, and Madison opened her eyes to glare at him. Which only made him laugh harder. Not because it was funny—more because it was so familiar.

"Well, what does your brother like?" Madison shot at him.

That stopped Luke's laugh. "I don't know," he confessed. "Maybe . . ." But he had nothing.

They both sat silently for a few minutes. Then Madison threw her hands in the air. "Well, this is ridiculous. And a waste of time. I'll just go home and do some research and figure something out."

Luke shook his head. "No, *I'll* do some research."

Madison raised a doubtful eyebrow, and Luke pushed his chair back. "Believe it or not, I do know how to use the internet."

Madison laughed, and Luke let go of the prickly feeling. But only a little bit.

"We'll both do some research, then," she said. "Text me with what you find. I'm sure we'll come up with something."

"Sounds good." Luke stood and pulled on his jacket and hat, then gathered up his empty pie plate as well as hers. She grabbed the mugs.

They deposited them on the counter, then headed for the door. As they reached it, he stepped ahead of her just enough to open it for her.

She gave him a surprised look. "Thanks."

He rolled his eyes. What did she think, that he wasn't sophisticated enough to know he should open the door for a lady?

The cold engulfed them the moment they stepped outside.

"I don't remember it being this cold in November when I used to live here." Luke hit his hands together.

"No. This is unseasonal. But the lights are pretty." Her breath fogged in front of her as she pointed to the Christmas lights lining the downtown storefronts. In the distance, occasional lights winked from the mountainsides surrounding the town as well.

"It's too early for Christmas decorations," he grumbled. "It's not even Thanksgiving yet."

"It's only a week and a half away," Madison pointed out. "I like when the lights are up early."

He shrugged. He'd be fine with skipping the whole holiday season.

"Well, goodnight." Madison pulled her jacket tighter around her and started across the parking lot. Luke squinted, but there wasn't a single car over there.

"Madicake?" he called.

"Don't call me that." But she turned around, the Christmas lights giving her a soft glow.

"Where are you going?"

"Back to the clinic. I left my car there."

"Are you crazy? It's freezing out. Come on. I'll give you a ride."

"It's only five blocks," she called back.

"Five blocks is plenty of time to turn into an icicle. How would I ever explain to your family why I had to bring you home in a block of ice?"

"My mother wouldn't let you bring me inside. I might melt on the floor," Madison said wryly.

"So you'll take a ride?"

"Fine." She threw her hands in the air. "Only because standing out here arguing with you has taken longer than walking would have, and my feet are already frozen."

He grinned, feeling as if he'd won some great contest, then moved to the passenger door of his truck to open it for her.

"Thank you." This time, there was no surprise in her voice.

"You're welcome." He closed the door, then hurried around to his side to turn on the vehicle and crank up the heat, thankful the engine was still warm enough that it didn't blast them with ice-cold air.

"Mmm. That feels nice." Madison closed her eyes and rested her head on the headrest.

Luke backed the truck out of the parking spot and steered toward the vet office.

"Do you always drive this slowly?" Madison cracked her eyes open, her lips quirked in a curious grin.

"Safety first," Luke said. But he pushed his foot a little harder to the gas. He hadn't been paying attention to his speed. He'd been too busy thinking about how different things could have been if . . .

He pushed the thought away. He'd made the choices he'd made. She'd made the choices she'd made. And there was no scenario in which those choices would have lined up.

He pulled into the parking lot at the vet and parked his truck right next to the only one left in the lot—a Volkswagen that was at least a decade old, if he wasn't mistaken. Not exactly the kind of car he'd pictured her in.

So she worked with animals and drove a Volkswagen. Maybe she *had* changed.

"Thanks for the ride." Madison pushed her door open. "You'll text me."

It wasn't a question, but Luke nodded. "I'll text you."

Chapter 4

Madison squinted at her checklist for the Santa Paws Pictures fundraiser. Had she really just checked off the last item on her to-do list?

"Woohoo!" The exclamation came out unbidden, and she grinned sheepishly to herself. Fortunately, Joseph was in an exam room with Mrs. Holland and her dog Pepper, who hadn't stopped barking since they'd arrived.

She did a mini victory dance in her seat. When she'd first suggested the fundraiser to Joseph, she hadn't really been sure she could pull it off. But he'd encouraged her to go for it—and now she'd done it.

She'd reserved the gazebo in the park, lined up refreshments for both the pets and their humans, even found someone to play Santa and have his picture taken with the animals—which of course Joseph's wife Ava would take. And they'd have a dog walk with fun stations for the pets and collect donations of food and supplies and money for the shelter in Brampton. It was going to be perfect.

She cast a guilty look at her clinical pathology textbook, shoved to the side of her desk. Santa Paws Pictures would be done after this weekend, and then she could focus on studying.

The sound of her cell phone vibrating called her attention to her purse, but she ignored it. Joseph didn't mind if she took personal calls during work, but she preferred not to. Besides, she'd be done in less than half an hour. Whoever it was could certainly wait that long.

The phone stopped buzzing, and Madison created a new spreadsheet to track donations so they could send out thank you cards after the event. But she'd just poised her fingers on the keyboard when the office phone rang.

"Good afternoon, River Falls Veterinary," she said cheerfully. "This is Madison. How can I help you?"

"Why didn't you answer your phone?" a woman's voice demanded.

"Hello to you too, Mel."

"Seriously, Madison. You're my maid of honor. I need to be able to reach you at a moment's notice."

"You did reach me," Madison pointed out.

"But I had to try twice. You know I'm busy."

Madison bit back a retort that she was busy too. "Okay, Mel. I'm sorry. What can I do for you?"

"I'm just calling to see how things are going with the plans for the Jack and Jill night."

"Oh, uh—" Madison drummed her fingers on her desk. "Good. Really good."

At least, she'd done a little bit of research, though she hadn't yet found something she thought Mel and Brad would like.

But it was more than Luke had done. It'd been three full days, and she hadn't gotten a single text from him.

Not that she was surprised. She'd known she'd be the one who ended up planning the whole thing. It just would have been nice if Luke had acknowledged that from the beginning. Then she wouldn't have wasted her time on that trip to Daisy's with him.

And she wouldn't have wasted so much time thinking about him afterward.

"Good," Mel continued. "We should really get together to discuss the details. Just so nothing slips through the cracks."

Madison rolled her eyes. "We don't need to meet, Mel. Nothing's going to slip through the cracks." She was already doing yet another search for what to do at a Jack and Jill party.

"Tonight? Dinner?" Mel continued as if Madison hadn't said a word.

"Can't we just talk about it at the engagement party on Saturday?"

"Don't be silly. I won't have time then. I'll be mingling. So dinner? Mazatlan?"

Madison sighed. She didn't know why she bothered to argue. She'd never been able to stand up to her big sister. "Isn't that in Brampton?" Madison had already driven there and back once today for school.

"Yeah, I'm at work now, and Bradley has to go in at eight. So if we do it at six, that should give us enough time. We'll meet you there. Okay. Bye."

Madison huffed as she pulled the phone away from her ear. So much for her plans to catch up on her homework tonight.

The phone rang again almost instantly. Madison gritted her teeth and forced herself to take a deep breath before she answered.

"River Falls Veterinary." She made herself smile so she'd sound pleasant. "This is Madison. How can I—"

"Did they call you too?"

"I'm sorry?" But it only took a moment for her brain to catch up with the voice.

Luke.

"Nice of you to text me," she said dryly.

"Yeah, nice of you to text me too," he shot back.

"Well, I—" Madison stuttered. She'd thought about it once or twice. But it had felt . . . weird. Besides, he'd clearly said he'd text her. Not the other way around.

"Anyway." Luke seemed to brush the comment aside. "I guess we're going to dinner together tonight. I can pick you up in fifteen minutes. That should give us just enough time to get there."

"I— Fifteen minutes?" Heat warmed Madison's face, and she waved at it impatiently. Who said they were driving together? "I can just meet you there."

"That would be silly," Luke said, in that oh-so-casual, oh-so-infuriating way he had. "There's no point in both of us wasting the gas. Besides, we can use the drive over to come up with something. Unless you already have?"

"As a matter of fact . . ." Madison scrolled down the screen in front of her, scanning the list in desperation. But there was nothing new here. And nothing she could picture her sister enjoying. "No," she admitted, though it nearly killed her.

"All right, then. Fifteen minutes. You'll be ready."

Madison glanced at the clock. It was 4:45 now. "Fine. You'll have to pick me up at work."

"Can do."

This time, as Madison pulled the phone away from her ear, a flutter worked its way up from her stomach.

No.

She dropped the phone onto the receiver and shook her head. She was absolutely *not* looking forward to spending more time with Luke.

Chapter 5

Luke drummed his hands on the steering wheel, keeping time to the music. He shook his head at himself. He shouldn't be in a good mood. He'd had a crummy day, with a customer who insisted Luke was gouging him on the price, even though he'd barely charged more than cost for the oxygen sensor he'd put in.

And his brother's call hadn't improved his mood.

In fact, he didn't think he'd cracked a smile all day. Until he'd gotten on the phone with Madison.

He shook his head again, harder this time, as if he could dislodge the image of her that had taken a seat right in the middle of his brain.

Once again, he tried to think of something else. The cold—no, that made him think of giving her a ride to her car the other night. The Mustang—no, that brought back old memories of her telling him Mustangs were her favorite car. The Christmas lights on the buildings—no, that brought him back to the other night.

He blew out a breath. Apparently, all roads led to Madison—at least in his brain.

He pulled into a front-row spot in the nearly empty parking lot of the vet clinic and got out of his car, inhaling a deep breath of the night air. It smelled of pine needles and cold, and his heart lifted. He'd missed this. Georgia had been fine. But it hadn't been the Smokies.

He paused at the clinic's glass door, letting himself watch Madison for a moment. She was on the phone, her hands animated as she talked, and he felt his lips pull into a smile, despite his best efforts to play it cool.

He opened the door and stepped into the warmth of the reception area. Twinkling Christmas lights traced the edges of the ceiling as well as the front of Madison's reception desk. Somehow he couldn't hate them when they surrounded her.

Madison looked up as the door closed and waved him forward without a smile.

"Yes, I understand, but I called weeks ago and I was told you had someone available." Madison sounded business-like but slightly desperate.

Luke moved closer, suddenly wanting to protect her from whatever the problem was. He leaned against the counter, watching Madison for a moment, but she turned her chair slightly so that her back was half to him.

He let his eyes scan the room, until they fell on a picture of a man with two dogs. Luke froze. He was pretty sure he knew that man. His smile dropped.

"Well, I guess if you can't, you can't." Madison's voice pulled his eyes back to her. "Thanks anyway."

She hung up the phone and dropped her head into her hands.

"Hey." Luke leaned as close as he could with the counter between them. "Is everything all right?"

Madison looked up, her glare driving him backwards. "No, it's not all right. I had everything lined up for the fundraiser and now . . . Joseph!" she turned and called over her shoulder.

Luke tensed.

What was he even doing here? He should have let her drive herself.

A moment later, the man from the picture emerged from the back room, wearing a pair of blue scrubs that should have made him look ridiculous but instead made him look like, well, a doctor.

Because that's what he is.

A little more impressive than a mechanic. A lot more Madison's type. As she'd made clear years ago.

Joseph Calvano hurried toward the desk, his brow wrinkled in concern. "Is everything all right?"

"Well," Madison answered him sweetly—without the glare she'd treated Luke to. "I'm not sure. That was the rental place. They double-booked. Which means we have no Santa. Are you sure one of your brothers can't do it?"

Joseph shook his head and raised a hand to smooth his already perfect hair. Luke noticed the wedding band on his finger. He'd already noticed the other day that Madison didn't wear one.

"I asked them all already. They have other plans. Dad too."

"Why don't *you* do it?" Luke had only the slightest idea what they were talking about. But from what he gathered, Madison needed someone to be Santa, and Luke didn't mind imagining Joseph looking ridiculous in a Santa suit.

"Oh sorry." Joseph looked up. "I didn't see you there."

Luke snorted quietly. It wasn't like he'd been hiding.

"Dr. Calvano can't do it." Madison said, and Luke wondered if she put an emphasis on the *doctor* or if it was only his imagination. "He's going to be doing free check-ups all day."

Oh, well, excuse him. Luke should have realized that Mr. Perfect would be too busy being perfect to don a Santa suit.

"But . . ." Madison turned to Luke, looking him up and down. He thought about making a joke about not being a piece of meat but bit it back.

"What are you doing on Saturday?" Madison asked.

"No," Luke answered flatly.

"No, what?" Madison asked innocently.

"No, I will not be your Santa."

"Please, Luke." Madison stood and leaned toward him, folding her hands on the counter right in front of him. Close enough that Luke could have wrapped his hands around them. If he'd wanted to.

He dug his hands deeper into his coat pocket, gripping the lining for extra assurance that they wouldn't do something stupid.

He shook his head. "Nope. Not in a million years. I don't even like Christmas."

Madison looked surprised. "You don't? Since when?"

Luke shook his head. Since Christmas had brought him some of the worst memories of his life. Like the look of disappointment on his wife's face when he got her the "wrong" present again. Or the way she'd rush out of the house for a "work emergency" the moment they'd finished unwrapping gifts. It wasn't until it had happened two years in a row that Luke had grown suspicious. Worse than that, Cindy hadn't even denied the affair with her boss when he'd asked. Instead, she'd presented him with divorce papers. But he didn't need to get into any of that. "Why do you need a Santa anyway?"

"So we can take pictures of the pets with him. It's the whole draw for the event."

"What event?"

"Madison organized a fundraiser to benefit the shelter," Joseph said, the warmth in his voice irking Luke.

"A lot of good it will do if no one comes." Madison sighed, picking up the phone.

"We'll figure it out tomorrow." Joseph's voice was soothing. "For now, you go do your thing with your sister and . . . Luke, right? You graduated a couple years ahead of us?"

Joseph held out a hand, and Luke shook it, gripping maybe a little harder than he had to.

"Yeah." He let go and turned to Madison. "You ready?"

She bit her lip. "I really don't think I can go. I'll have to call Mel. I only have two days to find someone . . ."

"Fine. I'll be Santa." What on earth? How had his mouth even opened? But he wasn't going to handle this dinner on his own, and if volunteering to be Santa was the only way to get Madison to come . . .

Madison and Joseph both looked at him, their mouths in identical circles.

"You will?" Madison finally asked.

"I—" He'd completely lost his mind. "I'll be your backup. You can make some calls tomorrow. I'm sure you'll find someone. But if you don't—" He groaned internally even as the words came out. "I'll do it."

"Hey, thanks man, that's great." Joseph's smile was warm.

"Yeah, sure," Luke mumbled, as if Joseph had anything to do with his offer. "Now, can we go?" he asked Madison. "We're going to be late the way it is."

"Yes, we can." Madison grinned at him, and it was almost worth the ridiculous promise he'd made. "See you tomorrow." She waved to Joseph as she rounded the desk.

Luke didn't bother saying goodbye as he hurried to open the door for her.

Outside, he ushered her to his truck, opening the passenger door. She slid in with an easy smile, and Luke closed the door gently behind her.

You're an idiot, he told himself as he strode to his side of the vehicle. Madison Monroe had always had the power to make him do crazy things. But offering to be Santa? That was the craziest by far.

He'd just have to count on the fact that she'd find someone else to-morrow. Because there was no way he was actually going to go through with this.

"How was your day?" Madison asked as he got into his seat and cranked up the heat for her.

"It was . . ." All the grouchy customers he'd dealt with seemed to fade. "Good. How was yours?"

"Exhausting." She laughed. "But good. I never realized how much I'd love this job."

That soured his mood. "You didn't mention you work for Joseph Calvano."

"Well, he *is* the only vet in town."

"What about Dr. Gallagher?"

"He retired. Joseph bought his practice."

Oh, now it was *Joseph* instead of Dr. Calvano?

"I seem to remember you had a giant crush on him." Luke couldn't hold the words back.

"On Dr. Gallagher?" Madison's voice held the trace of a laugh. "He was like ninety years old."

Luke glanced at her, trying to determine if she was putting him off. He couldn't tell. "On Joseph," he clarified.

"Oh." Madison shrugged. "I mean, for a little while. We went to prom together, but . . ." Her shoulders lifted in a shrug.

Luke tensed. He hadn't known that. But then, he'd already moved to Georgia to work in his uncle's shop by the time she had her senior prom. Actually, that had to have been right around the time he'd met Cindy.

"And now you work for him," he said.

"Yep."

"He's married," Luke blurted, unsure if it was a question or a statement.

"Yeah." Madison seemed unperturbed. "His wife is a photographer. She'll be taking your picture at the Santa Paws fundraiser."

"*If* you don't find anyone else," Luke added quickly.

"Right."

"Are you, uh—" The word *married* almost slipped out, followed by *seeing someone*, but he managed to hold his tongue on both. "Too hot?" He reached to turn down the heat on his side of the vehicle.

"I'm good, thanks. We should figure out what we're going to tell Brad and Mel. What do you think about karaoke?"

Luke laughed before he realized she was serious. "Sorry."

"What's wrong with karaoke?" He could hear the pout in her voice—not the whiny kind of pout Cindy had turned on when she wanted things her way. Madison's pout was sweeter, a little bit enticing—and a lot dangerous.

He did *not* need to be thinking of her as sweet *or* enticing.

"Nothing. But Brad has a terrible voice. So unless you want Mel to run away covering her ears . . ."

"Fine. I assume you have a better idea?" The pout had been replaced by a challenge, and Luke found he liked it even better.

Especially since he had an answer that would easily top karaoke. "How about the opera?"

He heard Madison shift in her seat and glanced her way to find her eyes on him.

"What?" he asked. "You have a problem with the opera?"

"No. I just wouldn't have pegged you as the opera type."

He grimaced. "Because I'm not cultured enough for the opera?"

"No. I was going to say you're not boring enough for the opera."

Luke laughed. "It's not boring. I promise. There are actually some really great stories."

"Okay, but when's the last time the opera came to River Falls?" she challenged.

"I was thinking we'd go to the Nashville Opera. They're doing La Bohème, and there are still tickets available. We could go out to dinner first, then go to the opera, and then stay overnight downtown." He stopped and waited for her response.

She'd either think he was a genius or think he was an idiot.

She didn't say anything, and he let his eyes go to her. She was staring straight ahead, but her lips curved up just the tiniest amount.

"So?"

She turned to him, and that little hint of a smile grew into an all-out laugh. "That might just work. It sounds like something Mel and Brad would love. Okay, so we'll need tickets, reservations for dinner—" She pulled out her phone and tapped away. She read out descriptions of a few restaurants, and amazingly, they agreed on one without any arguments.

"All right, now . . ." She tapped on her phone again. "Somewhere to stay. We'll need two rooms. One for the guys and one for the girls. Or maybe two for each. How many couples are there? I mean— Not that we're a—" she stammered. "People. How many people are in the wedding party?"

Luke chuckled to himself. "Well, there's you and me."

"Right," she murmured. "And Mel and Brad, obviously. I think Mel said there are three other girls, but one is from Utah, so I doubt she'll make it for this." She counted on her fingers. "Let's do four rooms, just in case."

"Or we could do two suites." He slowed to turn into the restaurant's driveway.

"Even better." Madison fell silent, tapping away on her phone. "There," she said jubilantly after a minute. "I think that might be the fastest I've ever planned anything."

"What do you mean, *you* planned?" Luke demanded, pulling into a parking spot.

Madison held up her phone. "Well, who made all the reservations?"

"Whose idea was it?" Luke shot back.

"All right, fine." Madison unbuckled her seatbelt. "I'll give you twenty percent of the credit."

"Twenty?" Luke scrambled out of his seat and around to her side of the truck to open her door. But he blocked her exit. "Fifty percent credit."

"Thirty percent," Madison countered.

Luke didn't budge.

"Luke." Madison shoved at his arm but instead of moving, he caught her hand.

It was warm and soft and wiggly. He gripped tighter. "Fifty-fifty."

Madison's eyes went to their hands. "Forty-sixty," she demanded, but he could tell she was weakening by the way she stopped trying to pull her hand away.

"Fifty. Fifty," he insisted. "Final offer."

"Fine." Madison laughed. "But only because we're late and if we don't get inside, Mel and Brad will probably fire us and then we'll have done all this planning for nothing."

"So, fifty-fifty?" He needed to confirm before he moved.

"Yes." She swung her legs out of the truck. "Now let me out."

He took a miniature step backwards, taking her hand with him and helping her down from her seat. But he hadn't moved back far enough, and she practically crashed into him.

He swallowed, holding her hand long enough to steady her before letting go and taking a larger step backwards.

She smiled at him, brushing a piece of hair off her forehead. "Brace yourself for this," she warned.

And even though he knew she was talking about the dinner with his brother and her sister, he realized he had to brace himself against something much more dangerous.

Her.

Chapter 6

"I can't believe her," Madison fumed as she passed Luke and stepped out of the stiff, stuffy restaurant. "You had a good idea. And we already made all the reservations and had everything all set up."

"She said it was fine." Luke jogged to catch up with her, his breath making her view of his face hazy as she turned to glare at him.

"Fine," she snorted. "Fine with Mel is like . . ." She sought for an apt comparison. "Is like . . . dirt for a worm."

"Worms like dirt," Luke pointed out.

Madison threw her arms in the air. "I don't know then. It's just . . . It's not good."

"Hey. It will be fine."

She snorted again. She was beginning to hate that word.

But Luke grabbed her arm and pulled her to a stop. She spun toward him, ready to fire off all the reasons it wouldn't be fine, but he took a step closer, and suddenly she couldn't remember a single one.

"It will be good," he said quietly. "I promise. And if they don't like it, too bad for them. We can still have fun."

"We can?" she breathed. He smelled like cedar and coffee and something warm she couldn't identify. She had to fight not to step closer.

"We *will*," he insisted. "Now come on. Before we freeze."

"You're the one who stopped me," she pointed out.

He snorted and grabbed her elbow, leading her to his truck.

He opened her door, and she let herself relax into the seat. Exhaustion swam over her, but she still had so much to do tonight. That lab procedures paper wasn't going to write itself, and those physiology notes she had to catch up on . . .

She massaged her temples.

Luke's door opened, and she heard him get into the vehicle. Heard the engine start.

"Are you okay?" His voice was oddly gentle as they began to back out.

Madison opened her eyes. "And did you catch what she said about the gift from the bridal party? I didn't realize we were all expected to go in on something together. I don't have time to set that up."

"I can do it," Luke offered.

"Really?" She hoped she didn't sound skeptical.

"Yeah. Really." He slowed for a stoplight. "I was thinking we could get them one of those giant singing fish. My uncle used to have one, and I thought it was the coolest thing."

Madison tried to hold back a laugh but failed. "That sounds great. And I'll even let you take one hundred percent credit for that."

"Good." Luke made a left turn, and Madison sat up, peering down the street.

This was not the way back to River Falls. "You weren't supposed to turn for a few streets yet."

"I know." Luke kept driving.

"So what are you doing? I need to get home." She glanced at the time. It was 7:30 now. Which meant she'd get home around 8:30. Which meant she'd have about four hours to study before she absolutely had to go to bed so she could get up for work tomorrow.

"You're stressed," Luke said.

She shook her head. No kidding she was stressed. And keeping her from getting home to study wasn't helping.

"Seriously, Luke. I have to get home."

"Hot date?"

She couldn't tell if he was joking or not. She thought about saying yes, just to see how he'd react. "No."

"Don't tell me it's past your bedtime," Luke quipped.

"I wish." Madison sighed. "I'm going to be up for hours yet."

"Doing what?" Luke held up a hand. "Don't tell me. Binging Hallmark Christmas movies."

"No. If you must know—" She broke off as Luke pulled into the parking lot of what appeared to be a drive-in restaurant. "What are you doing?"

"Helping you de-stress."

"I don't need to de-stress. I need to get home. And I'm still stuffed from dinner."

Ignoring her, Luke pulled up under the awning. Madison glanced at her phone. How long would it take to get home if she called a ride service?

But a bundled up waitress was already on the way to their spot. Luke rolled down his window. "Two hot chocolates please. To go."

Madison relaxed just a little. Getting it to go shouldn't take too long. And hot chocolate did sound nice.

"So, you were saying? About why you have to get home?" Luke broke into her thoughts.

"Nothing." Madison tucked her tongue between her teeth. He didn't need to know about her classes. He'd probably just make fun of her.

"I believe your exact words were, 'If you really need to know.'" Luke turned toward her, the overhead lights from the drive-in illuminating his smile.

"Yeah, well, you don't really need to know, so . . ."

"*Oh.*" Luke's eyebrows shot up. "Something illegal, maybe. Or something—"

"Study, okay. I have to study." Madison huffed out a breath. It wasn't fair that he'd always known how to push her buttons.

Luke's look changed from teasing to surprised. "Study what?"

She blew her hair out of her face. There wasn't much point in not answering. He'd just pester her until she caved. Again.

"I'm studying to be a vet tech. At the tech school here. In Brampton."

"Huh." Luke nodded. "That's cool."

"But . . ." Madison prompted.

Luke lifted an eyebrow. "No but."

Madison waited. If she told her family, there would be "buts" galore: *But you've started school three times before and never stuck with it. But a vet tech has to do all the dirty work. But you'll never be a doctor like your sister.*

The waitress bustled to Luke's window, handing in the hot chocolates. Luke passed Madison one, settling his own into the cupholder between them. He paid the waitress, then backed the truck out of their spot.

A little pinprick of disappointment stuck Madison, but she ignored it. She was the one who'd said they couldn't stay.

She took a tentative sip of her cocoa. "Mmm." She closed her eyes, letting the rich, full flavor warm her from the inside out.

"It's good?" Luke asked.

"Maybe the best I've ever had. Thank you."

"You're welcome." He sounded satisfied. "And I really do think it's cool that you're going to be a vet tech. I'm sure you'll be great at it."

Madison blinked back a sudden, ridiculous prickling behind her eyelids. He was just being polite, and yet, it felt nice to have someone rooting for her.

Maybe it was time to change the subject. "So, you opened your own shop?"

"Yeah." Why did he sound so guarded suddenly?

"How's that going?"

"Good. The building itself needs some work. But we've had good business so far."

36

"That's great." She tried not to think of the summer he'd spent telling her about cars in between the time they spent swimming in the ocean. She'd been a smitten fifteen-year-old then. And he'd been oblivious.

"You're divorced?" Oops. She hadn't meant for that to pop out so abruptly. But Brad had said something about Luke's ex at dinner, and Madison hadn't wanted to ask about it then.

"Uh huh." It was more of a grunt than an answer.

Madison tried to take the hint, she really did. But she had to know. "How long were you married?"

"Four and a half years."

She waited for him to elaborate, to say something about his wife, about what had happened, about . . . something.

When he didn't, she drained the rest of her hot cocoa.

But when she moved to set the empty cup in the cupholder, Luke's hand was already there.

"Oh. Sorry." A barrage of fireworks popped against Madison's skin as she pulled her fingers back.

"That's okay." Luke's voice was strained. "Go ahead." He shifted his hand to the side, and Madison settled her cup into its spot, then tucked her hands into her lap. Luke kept his hand wrapped around the cup between them.

"So what does a vet tech do?" he asked.

"Oh, well—" Madison adjusted in her seat, feeling an odd sense of excitement at the opportunity to talk about it. She talked to Joseph about her classes, of course, but he already knew all of it—and plenty more.

Luke, on the other hand, was genuinely curious. He listened and asked questions and made it so easy for her to talk about that she was surprised when he pulled into the clinic parking lot. She was just telling him about her fear of having to help put animals down.

"I'm sure you'll be great at it." Luke pulled up next to her car and slid the gear into park.

Madison snorted. "I'm not sure that's a compliment."

"That came out wrong." Luke turned and looked at her earnestly. "I mean, you'll be great at comforting the pets' owners."

"Oh." Madison swallowed. The vehicle felt like it had suddenly shrunk to matchbox size. "I hope so." She had a hard time tearing her eyes away from his.

"So, uh, goodnight." Luke's Adam's apple bobbed.

She nodded. "Yeah. Goodnight." She opened her door and stepped into the chilly air. "Don't forget about Saturday. Santa." She grinned at him. "I'll have your costume ready."

"Only if you don't find anyone else." Luke glowered, but she was pretty sure she could detect a smile under it.

"Of course." She closed the door with a laugh and unlocked her car, already missing the warmth of Luke's truck. Already missing . . .

No. She wasn't missing his company.

She got into her car and glanced over to find he was still there, watching her. She fumbled her keys, her hands suddenly a little shaky. But she managed to jab the key in the ignition and start the engine.

Luke waved for her to pull out first.

She let out a breath that fogged in front of her face, then put the car in reverse.

A moment later, Luke followed, turning left out of the parking lot when she turned right.

She reached to crank up the heat, wincing as it blasted cold air into her face.

The car made a strange sound, and she could have sworn it said, *You needed that.*

But she didn't. She already knew that no matter how pleasant the evening had been, it didn't mean anything.

Luke had made it clear years ago that he saw her as nothing more than a silly little girl.

She thought of the way he'd reacted to her announcement that she was studying to be a vet tech. The way he'd listened.

He hadn't seemed to think she was silly. In fact, he'd seemed rather . . . impressed.

But that didn't mean she'd ever be more than some girl he kissed for a laugh one Christmas.

Or that he'd ever be more than the guy she used to have a crush on—heavy emphasis on the *used to*.

Chapter 7

"You didn't make a single other call, did you?" Luke grumbled as he climbed the steps of the Founder's Park gazebo, where Madison was adding fake snow around a throne-like chair. The temperature had warmed after the recent cold spell, and the sky was that brilliant shade of blue he'd taken for granted until he'd moved away.

Madison turned and met him with a glittering smile that was brighter than the sun—and made him warmer too. The elf hat perched on her head jingled cheerfully, and he couldn't really stay mad. But he could at least keep up appearances. He crossed his arms over his chest.

"I made some calls, I promise," Madison said. "I had to call around to find a Santa suit."

"You—" Luke sputtered. "That wasn't what I meant. Did you even ask anyone else to do this?"

"I plead the fifth."

"That wasn't the deal," Luke huffed. Obviously, he couldn't tell her that he'd been hoping she wouldn't find anyone else.

"This looks like it was a lot of work." He scanned the area around the gazebo, which had been turned into a village of doggy houses all decked out for Christmas. In the middle of them was a large Christmas tree decorated in bone-shaped ornaments.

"It was." Madison adjusted a wrapped gift box, then stood, brushing her hands together. "There. I think we're ready." Her eyes came to him.

"Almost." She zipped over to a bench along the gazebo's edge and swooped up a fuzzy red pile with something white and fluffy on top.

She hurried back, holding it out to him.

Luke took the pile, pinching the fluffy white mass between his fingers. "You don't really expect me to wear this do you?"

"Oh yes, I do," Madison replied crisply. "Who ever heard of a beardless Santa?"

"It's for dogs. They're not going to know the difference."

Madison glared at him. "Put it on. Now. People are starting to show up."

Luke tried to stare her down, but someone called her name, and she bustled off.

He watched her go, admiring the way her hair bounced around her shoulders and her laugh carried behind her.

Okay, costume. He forced himself to sort through the pieces, mostly so he'd have something else to concentrate on.

He tugged the red pants on over his jeans, then eyed what looked like a backpack stuffed with a pillow. He groaned—that must be to give him the characteristic Santa belly. Reluctantly, he pulled it on over his stomach and wrapped the large red coat around his shoulders. He sized up the beard and wig. Would anyone really notice if he didn't wear them?

Madison would.

He grimaced but grabbed the beard and pulled the strap around his head, arranging the uncomfortable material around his mouth and nose so that he could at least breathe. Then he pulled the wig over his scalp, tucking his hair under it the best he could. He jammed the Santa hat on top of it.

A bead of sweat trickled down his back, followed by another. Of course it had to be warmer today than it had been in weeks.

Madison was going to owe him. Big time.

He scanned the park looking for her. He still had no idea what he was supposed to do now that he'd put this contraption on.

There. She was standing at a table chatting with Joseph and a woman Luke didn't recognize. He started toward them, his movements awkward in the bulky suit.

He had made it to the bottom of the gazebo stairs when the two women broke away and started toward him.

Luke registered the exact moment Madison caught sight of him because her eyes widened and her hand slapped over her mouth—but it wasn't enough to hide her laughter.

"That's it," Luke called. "I'm out of here."

"No, Luke. I'm sorry." Madison hurried forward, her eyes still full of mirth. "You look great. I just never realized what a perfect Santa you would make, that's all." She gestured to the woman who had come up behind her. "This is Ava, Dr. Calvano's wife."

"It was so nice of you to come to our rescue," Ava said, holding out a hand to him with a warm smile. One side of her face was wrinkled in what looked like scar tissue—maybe from a burn, though Luke couldn't be sure. "We all appreciate it."

"I chalk it up to being in the wrong place at the wrong time," Luke said wryly. "So what exactly am I supposed to do?"

"Just sit on the chair—" Madison gestured to the throne. "And the dogs will sit next to you or in your lap—or whatever Ava tells them to do. All you have to do is smile, and she'll take your picture."

"No one will see me smile under this thing." Luke tugged on his beard.

"Fine. Then you can frown if you want to."

"Good." But his lips refused to drop into a frown.

Fortunately, there was no way for Madison to see that.

"I have to go make sure everything is set up for the Canine Christmas Walk. I'll check on you in a bit." She started to walk away but then spun on her heel, her hair swinging behind her. "I almost forgot." She held out a bag. "Here are some treats to give them when they're done." He took the bag, but she didn't start on her way again. Instead, she stared for a moment, then took a step forward, her hand darting out and sweeping across his forehead.

He startled, pulling back.

"Hold still." Madison's eyes came to his. "Some of your hair is sticking out."

"Oh." He caught his breath as her fingers tucked his hair under the wig. She smelled like vanilla and gingerbread and everything warm and cozy he'd ever smelled.

"There." She gave a satisfied nod and stepped back, and he could breathe again. "Have fun." She waved and was off.

"Let's get a couple of practice shots." Ava lifted her camera. "I want to make sure I have all my settings right. Taking pictures of animals can be challenging."

"Sure." Luke moved to take his seat. "Why does Santa have a throne?" he asked, more to himself than to Ava.

But she laughed. "Because it was in my prop room. It was either that or a bathtub, so you're welcome."

Luke laughed along with her but let his eyes wander to where Madison had stopped to talk to a young family with two boys and a dog. She bent over to listen to something one of the boys was saying, then threw her head back in a laugh before ruffling the boy's hair.

A strange pang went through Luke.

When he'd asked Cindy to marry him, he'd figured that by now they'd have a kid or two, along with a dog. But Cindy kept saying she wasn't ready for children. The dog she'd agreed to—and taken in the divorce.

"It looks like we have our first customer," Ava called.

Luke tore his gaze away from Madison—and it landed on a giant, drooling St. Bernard.

He barely held back his groan. It was going to be a long morning.

"Hey, Madison. You might want to get over to the gazebo. Mrs. Hoff's dog just mistook your Santa for a tree." Tamara, from Madison's physiology class, hurried over to her, barely hiding a snicker.

"He what?" Madison covered her mouth in horror—and maybe to stifle a small giggle.

Tamara raised her eyebrows. "You heard me right."

Madison jogged toward the gazebo, relieved to find that Luke was still up there. It couldn't have been that bad if he hadn't run away.

She eyed the line of people still waiting to get their pets' photos taken with him. It was going to be hard to get them all done in the fifteen minutes before the event was supposed to end.

Rather than pushing her way through the crowd, she circled around the back of the gazebo and climbed the steps, hanging back to let Luke finish up with his current customer—a Dalmatian she recognized as belonging to the Carruth family. Their little girl Tabitha had recently gone through chemo, but she looked like she was doing well. Her eyes sparkled as she watched Luke squat down next to the dog and wrap an arm around its neck.

"Smile, Paisley," the girl called, and as if on cue, the dog turned and gave Luke's cheek a big lick.

The girl's giggle was huge and contagious and Madison found her eyes going to Luke as his laugh burst out louder than any of them.

"You want to be in a picture too?" he asked the girl.

The girl nodded but then seemed to develop a case of bashfulness, tucking her chin to her neck and remaining rooted to her spot.

"It's okay," her mom urged. "Go ahead."

Luke dropped all the way to his knees, and Madison tried not to let her heart get caught up in the way he held out a hand to the girl. "Come on. You can help me give Paisley a treat when we're done."

The girl smiled at that and sped up her steps a little. When she got to Luke, she dropped to kneel on the ground next to him. He gently rested an arm around her shoulder, his other arm still around the dog.

Madison swallowed. That was so not fair. She absolutely had no desire to revisit her once-upon-a-time crush on the man. But seeing him like this was pulling on every heartstring she owned.

Ava snapped a few more pictures, then Luke stood and held out a hand to help the girl up. He pulled a treat out of his pocket and handed it to her. She giggled as she fed it to the dog, then spun and wrapped her arms around Luke's waist before running back to her parents with a giggle.

Luke still looked slightly stunned as Madison took the opportunity to sneak up next to him.

"Everything going okay?" she asked.

Luke looked at her in surprise. "Yeah. Great." He turned to watch the Carruths clamber down the gazebo steps as the next pet—Mr. Germain's chocolate lab Cocoa—charged up them with a record-breaking level of energy.

"She hugged me." Luke sounded slightly amazed.

Madison laughed, mostly because it was either that or hug him herself. "I saw. She's a sweet kid. She was in treatment for cancer."

Luke spun toward her. "Is she okay?"

Madison nodded. "Last I heard, yes."

"I can't even imagine," Luke murmured, and it suddenly occurred to Madison that he might have children of his own.

Before she could ask, Cocoa was nearly bowling them over.

Luke dropped to his knees, wrapping his arms around the dog and scratching behind its ears.

Cocoa leaned into him as if they were best friends. "You're a good boy, aren't you?" Luke said to the dog, turning for Ava to take their picture.

Madison backed quickly out of the way.

It looked like she needn't have worried about Luke.

"Listen, the line is still pretty long," she said as Luke gave Cocoa his treat. "I think we probably have time for about three or four more. I'll let everyone after that know we won't get to them. I don't want them to waste their last few minutes waiting in line."

Luke frowned. "Do we have to be out of here by a certain time?"

"Well . . . no," Madison said slowly. "But technically the event ends at eleven."

"I can stay," Luke said. "Until we get through everyone. If that works for you," he added, looking to Ava.

"Of course," Ava replied. "That's a great idea." She gave Madison a look that said she thought Madison was the reason for Luke's generosity.

Madison shook her head. "You really don't have to—"

But Luke turned to her, and though the fluffy beard hid his mouth, she could see the smile in his eyes. "I'm not going to be the Santa who ruined Christmas for those families." He readjusted his Santa hat. "Besides, this way you'll owe me even bigger."

Madison shoved his arm—more surprised than she should have been at how firm it was under the thick suit. She pulled her hand back. "I'm going to go help with the cleanup from the walk. Thank you."

"No problem." Luke was already holding out his hands to take the next pet—Mrs. Bernelli's teacup chihuahua Lacy. The moment it was in his arms, it growled.

"Oh. That's how it's going to be, huh?" Luke readjusted the dog, which growled again.

Madison allowed herself to watch for a moment, and Luke's eyes came to hers. She froze but then turned and spun toward the back steps.

She had to make her escape before Luke changed his mind about staying to get everyone's pictures.

And before she changed hers—about not redeveloping her crush on him.

Chapter 8

Luke peeled off the Santa suit, trying not to think about just how sweaty the back of his t-shirt must be by now.

"I see you decided to stick with the bearded look." Madison jogged up the steps, grinning at him in a way that made his heart do things it wasn't supposed to do.

"Do you like it?" He ran a hand over the white fuzz, as if he were a wizened sage.

She laughed, her eyes sparkling. "You did a great job. Everyone loved you."

Oh, man. Those words should not make his insides light up the way they did.

"There were a lot of dogs." He tried to sound grumpy. She didn't need to know how much fun he'd had.

"You're not fooling me." Madison pointed at him. "You're totally a dog person."

Luke shrugged. "I never said I wasn't. But that doesn't mean you don't owe me. Big time."

"Wow, Madison. That was incredible." Joseph smiled at her as he and Ava approached arm in arm. "Everyone I talked to loved it. I don't know how you managed to pull it all together, but I'd say this will become an annual event."

"Thanks." Madison seemed to glow under Joseph's praise, and Luke felt his own mood sour. He could have told Madison the same thing.

So why didn't you?

He pulled off the wig and beard, running a hand through his damp hair.

"I think you've found yourself a permanent gig as Santa, if you want it." Ava smiled at him, but Luke shook his head.

"This was a one-time deal. Emergency situation only."

"We'll see about that." Madison grinned at him, and suddenly Luke thought it wouldn't be such a bad thing if they needed an emergency Santa again next year.

"Do y'all want to get some lunch?" Madison asked.

"Sorry, we have to take off." Ava leaned over to hug Madison. "This was fun though."

"See y'all later." Joseph gave Madison a look Luke couldn't interpret, and his stomach tightened. Were those the kinds of looks he hadn't caught between Cindy and her boss?

He pushed the thought aside. Joseph was clearly happy in his marriage. Unlike, apparently, Cindy.

"What about you?" Madison turned to him, her eyes still bright.

"What about me?"

"Do you want to get some lunch?" She sounded slightly breathless.

"Oh. Uh—"

"You did say I owe you," Madison pointed out.

"And you think lunch will make us even?" He raised an eyebrow. "Might I remind you that I've been wearing a Santa costume—complete with wig, beard, and belly—" He nudged the pack with his toe. "For three hours."

Madison laughed. "Well, at least you looked cute doing it." Her smile dropped into a mortified O shape.

Luke laughed to cover the current that surged through him like the sudden zap of a spark plug. She thought he was cute? "I didn't realize you were attracted to Santa."

Madison's face went from warm glow to fiery furnace. "I never said I was attracted to you. I said you were cute. I mean—" She stuttered, and Luke felt his smile grow. "I mean as Santa. You were cute as—" She broke off with a head shake. "I'm going to shut up now."

"No, don't." Luke touched her arm. "You're cute when you're flustered." He let the words hang there, not qualifying them. Not trying to take them back or cover them up.

"I'm not flustered." Madison deftly slid her arm out of his grip. "I'm just . . . exhausted. It was a lot of work to plan all of this."

"You did a great job," Luke said quietly.

"Thanks." Madison looked away. "I should get going."

"Wait. What about lunch?"

She crossed her arms in front of her. "I thought you said that wasn't enough to pay you back."

"It's not." He bent to pick up the pieces of the Santa suit. "But it's a start."

Madison played with a French fry, keeping her eyes on the crowds buzzing in and out of Murf's. But she was way too aware of Luke sitting across from her. Of the way their knees almost touched under the small table. Of the way his hair stuck up just a little bit from pulling off that Santa wig earlier. Of the way she wanted to reach over and smooth it down, not because it bothered her—but because she suddenly had the most ridiculous urge to touch him.

She shoved the fry into her mouth, then took a long sip of milkshake.

Luke picked up his cheeseburger. "As good as I remember."

Madison nodded. It was safest to assume he was talking about the food.

"So, you like dogs." It was the first topic of conversation her brain landed on. "Do you have one?"

Luke's face darkened.

"My wife got him in the divorce."

"Oh. I'm sorry. What kind was he?"

"Yellow lab."

"Are you going to get another one? The shelter always has dogs who need a home. Here, let me give you their number." She pulled out her phone, but Luke held up a hand.

"Hold on. Hold on. I didn't say yes. I'm not home enough and—"

"Bring him to work. People love that." She scrolled through her contacts. "Give me your phone."

He passed it to her, and she opened his contacts, entering the number of the shelter until an incoming text notification blocked her view of the screen.

Instinctively, her eyes skimmed it. *Is she hot?*

Her gaze flicked to Luke. Was who hot? She glanced back at the screen to check who had sent the text, but it had already disappeared. She made herself finish adding the contact info. Had the questioner been asking about *her*? Or was Luke seeing someone? Or . . .

She thrust his phone back at him.

It didn't matter who the text had been about. She didn't care. Not one little bit.

She shoved another fry into her mouth.

"Did you get your studying done the other night?" Luke's question caught her by surprise.

She groaned. "I don't want to talk about it. I was up until 2 a.m. studying, and then I got to the test and I forgot everything. I'm sure I bombed it."

"I'm sure you didn't." Luke stole one of her fries. "When do you graduate?"

"Assuming I pass? In the spring." She sighed. Sometimes this whole thing felt bigger than her.

"And then what?" Luke asked. "Keep working for Dr. Calvano?" His voice hardened at Joseph's name, and Madison wondered what was up with that. It was clear he didn't like Joseph—but what wasn't clear was why. Joseph was probably the nicest man anyone had ever met.

"That's the plan, yes." She finished off her milkshake. "He gave me a job when no one else would, even though I had next to no experience. And now that his practice is growing, he really does need a tech."

Luke shoved the last bite of his burger into his mouth without comment. Madison finished her meal as well, and there really was no reason to stay any longer.

"I should get home and study for a bit before the engagement party tonight."

"And I should shower." Luke stood and gathered up their mess. "That Santa suit was *toasty*."

"Thank you again for doing that." Madison let herself touch his arm for a moment. "I really do appreciate it."

"I know you do." Luke's smile was warm but mischievous. "And your debt to me is one-fifth paid."

"One-fifth?" Madison raised a brow. "You really think your service as Santa was worth five times lunch?"

Luke nodded solemnly. "I do."

"Well, what can I do to pay back the other four-fifths?"

"Oh, don't worry." Luke grinned at her. "I'll come up with something." He held the door open for her and they walked together to their vehicles, which were parked side by side. But neither of them made a move toward their doors.

"So." Luke looked at her. "I guess I'll see you later."

"I guess you will." Madison made herself get into her car, trying not to look forward to later.

Chapter 9

Madison pressed her foot to the gas as hard as she dared. The last thing she needed was for Zeb Calvano to pull her over right now. He'd let her off with a warning last time only because she'd been on her way to help his brother deliver a litter of puppies. But she was pretty sure he wouldn't be as lenient about speeding to get to her sister's engagement party.

She'd promised Mom she'd be there early, but then she'd gotten caught up working on her veterinary nutrition paper and completely lost track of time. And now she was going to be at least half an hour late.

Mom hadn't called yet, but that wasn't necessarily a good sign. It only meant Madison was going to get the you-don't-care-enough-to-be-on-time cold shoulder.

A hundred feet ahead of her, the lights at the railroad crossing flashed to life and the gates came down. Madison groaned. She could turn around and backtrack, but that would take at least another twenty-five minutes—and there was no guarantee she'd beat the train to the next stop. Better to wait it out. Mom and Dad's house was only ten minutes on the other side of the tracks.

She pulled up to the crossing and put her car in park, grabbing the physiology book she'd stuck into her bag just in case she found a spare moment to study tonight. She turned on the overhead light and opened the book—but her thoughts kept drifting back to the fundraiser this morning and to lunch and—most infuriatingly—to Luke. To the way he'd hugged the dogs and laughed with the kids. To the way he'd listened to her and encouraged her.

She'd managed to push it off most of the day, but suddenly that childhood crush was roaring back at her as powerfully as the train was roaring down the tracks in front of her.

And if she wasn't mistaken, Luke had shown signs of feeling it too.

But you are *mistaken*, she reminded herself.

Which was why she wasn't about to throw herself at him again. Although, if he happened to ask her out, she might not say no.

The end of the train came into sight, and Madison snapped her book shut with a sigh. She was supposed to be focusing on her studies and her career, not some unrequited crush.

She shoved the book into her bag and shifted into drive as the crossing gates lifted. Ten minutes later, she was pulling up to her parents' house, resolved not to let her silly feelings distract her from what really mattered. Dozens of cars already lined the long driveway, and she had to work hard to ignore the jump in her stomach when she spotted Luke's truck at the back of the line. She pulled in behind it, grabbed her bag, and started the long trek toward the home she'd grown up in.

Though the house in front of her was grand, Madison couldn't resist pausing to look over her shoulder, down into the valley below. In the dark, the lights of River Falls twinkled up at her, while the stars glittered overhead, and an overwhelming sense of peace washed over Madison. "You're pretty amazing, Lord," she whispered as she turned to continue toward the house.

She paused at the double front doors, took a deep breath, and tried to hold onto that feeling of peace as she stepped inside.

"How nice of you to put in an appearance." Her mother barely let her get past the threshold before she swooped down on her.

"Sorry, Mom." Madison adjusted her bag on her shoulder. "I got caught up and lost track of time and then there was a—"

"Caught up with what?" But before Madison could answer, Mom was already steamrolling ahead. "It sure would be nice if you'd live up to your responsibilities once in a while. Go get some food. It's probably cold by now."

"That's okay. I'm not—" But Mom was already greeting a couple who had come in behind Madison.

Madison noticed they weren't scolded for being late. Nor were they offered cold food, as her mother assured them everything was still "piping hot."

Madison sighed and made her way toward the kitchen, scanning the crowd along the way. It was mostly her parents' friends, as well as some of Mel's high school friends and guys she imagined must be Brad's buddies. She spotted Mel and Brad chatting with Brad and Luke's parents. But where was—

There.

Her gaze landed on Luke—and the brunette he was laughing with. The woman touched Luke's arm, and he smiled, then angled his head just enough toward Madison that she jumped and turned away.

Now what?

She needed to look like she had a purpose—other than staring at him.

She strode toward the buffet her parents had catered in and filled a plate, barely paying attention to the foods she put on it.

How could she have been so stupid? Thinking there might be something between her and Luke. That her crush might not be one-sided. That he might actually ask her out—and she might say yes.

He hadn't been showing her special attention. He'd only been doing her a favor she'd had to beg him to do. And he'd only seen lunch with her as payback for that favor. Not as a chance to spend time with her.

She carried her plate back through the crowd to a spot as far away from Luke as she could find. The angle she was sitting at meant she had to crane her neck if she wanted to see him—which she didn't. Still, every time she accidentally torqued her head in that direction, he was with the same woman.

Once or twice, Madison almost convinced herself he was looking her direction, but she darted her gaze away too quickly to be sure. She didn't need him to think she was pining for him.

"Are these seats taken?"

Madison looked up to find her father's business partner Doug and his wife Sandy gesturing to the armchairs across from her.

"Of course not. Have a seat." Madison smiled and let herself be drawn into a conversation about their son Henry's studies at Harvard. It may not be the most entertaining way to spend the evening—but it was sure better than sitting here watching Luke flirt with another woman.

By the time Doug and Sandy excused themselves to mingle, Madison was thinking longingly of her bed. But there was no way she could duck out early after arriving late.

Still, no one would notice if she sneaked outside for a bit to get some air. She grabbed her bag and slid through the crowd, careful to avoid Luke and his new girlfriend, who were *still* talking.

Rather than using the French doors behind them, she slipped down the hallway to the door that led to the backyard from the den. She closed it silently behind her and crept to the stairs that dropped into the spacious backyard. With a sigh, she sank onto the top step and allowed herself a moment to breathe in the fresh mountain air. But it held a hint of cedar, which only made her think of Luke.

A gentle breeze rustled the few leaves that remained on the trees, and Madison pulled her hands into the sleeves of her sweater. After a few minutes, she made herself take out her physiology book and open it in her lap. Between the low lights on the deck and the moonlight, it was just bright enough to read. This time, Madison didn't let any ridiculous thoughts distract her—though that didn't keep them from trying. But she pushed through, and soon she was completely absorbed in a chapter on mitral insufficiency in dogs.

The thud of a door closing made her jump, and she slammed her book shut and stuffed it in her bag.

"Hope I'm not interrupting anything." Luke's voice held a chuckle, and she let out a sharp breath.

Don't let yourself fall back into crush mode.

"Nope." She wrapped her arms around her knees.

"Oh good. By the way you jumped, I thought maybe you were on some covert mission out here." He lowered himself to the step next to her—not close enough for their arms to touch, but close enough that she could enjoy the way his scent mingled with the night air. She wrapped her arms tighter so she wouldn't move closer.

"I was just sneaking in a couple minutes to study," she confessed.

"And you hid your book when I came out because you're afraid I'll operate on my own non-existent dog and put you out of business?"

She laughed, in spite of her resolution not to be charmed by him. "No. I thought you might be my mother."

"And your mom is opposed to studying?"

Madison shrugged. "She doesn't know."

"Doesn't know what?"

"That I'm in school. No one does. Except Joseph. And now you."

She could feel his eyes on her, but she kept hers on the ground in front of the deck.

"Why?" he finally asked.

She sighed and pushed her hands through her hair. "I don't know. I just— I feel like they'll blow it off, you know? Like it's just one more flaky 'Madison thing.'" She made air quotes around the expression her family had coined to describe her seemingly passing interests. "I've started and stopped school so many times. But this time, I know it's what I want to do. And I'm paying for it myself." She cut off. That had to sound like a stupid thing to say. She was twenty-seven years old. Of course she should be paying for it herself. Even if it took nearly every penny she made that didn't go to her rent and food. "I guess I just want to wait until I'm done and surprise them." And that way, if she failed, they'd never know.

"That's fair," Luke said simply. "And your secret is safe with me."

"Thanks." Madison accidentally met his eyes. In the dark, they looked deep and rich and— "So, I see you're as popular with the ladies as ever." She attempted a playful tone. It wasn't an accusation. Just an observation.

"What?" Luke's eyes crinkled adorably, as if he really was confused. "Oh, you mean London?"

Madison lifted a shoulder, wishing she hadn't brought it up.

"She was trying to sell me life insurance." Luke chuckled.

"She was not." Madison shoved his arm, the heat of his skin pulsing through his button-up. She jammed her hand back into her lap.

Luke laughed harder. "I swear, she was. Apparently I give off an old-man-about-to-kick-the-bucket vibe."

Madison snorted. "Right."

Luke shrugged. "She wanted to make sure my family would be protected if anything happened to me." His expression sobered. "I told her I didn't have any family."

"Oh." That answered Madison's question about whether he had any kids.

"And then she told me all the reasons I still need insurance," Luke added. "I tried to catch your eye so you could rescue me, but you were no help." He leaned close enough to bump his shoulder against hers. "So thanks for nothing."

"You're welcome." At least now she knew she hadn't imagined he was looking at her.

"Boy, being at your parents' house again brings back a lot of memories," Luke said abruptly.

"Yeah." Madison let her answer hang there, not asking what he meant. Which memories he was referring to. Their families had spent many Christmases together here. Including the one when they'd—

Nope. She was *not* going to relive their one and only kiss.

"Is it just me, or is it weird to think of Brad and Mel getting married?" Luke asked.

"Well, they have a lot in common," Madison pointed out. "They're both doctors, and . . ." She was sure there was more to it than that, but she didn't really spend enough time with them to know what.

"Yeah, I know." Luke stretched his legs down the length of the steps and rubbed his hands on his jeans. "But when we were kids, it was always you and I who hung out."

"Yeah." Madison swallowed.

"Do you think maybe—"

A door opened behind them, and they both jumped. "What are you two doing out here?" Mel called. "It's time for the toasts."

"Be right there," Luke said over his shoulder, but his eyes didn't leave Madison's.

"Hurry up." The door closed, and Luke stood, holding out a hand.

Madison set her hand in his, trying but failing to ignore the wild surge of her heart at the contact. Luke held on even after she was on her feet, and she almost asked what he'd been about to say before Mel interrupted.

"I guess we should go inside." He let go of her hand, and she nodded, following him into the house.

Chapter 10

"I don't see why we have to go to the tree lighting," Luke grumbled as he spooned the leftover cranberries into a container.

"Because we go every year," Mom said cheerfully, sliding plates into the dishwasher.

"I don't," Luke pointed out.

"But that's one of the great parts of being back home," Mom said. "You can participate in all our family traditions again."

"Hmph." Luke yanked the fridge open and shoved the cranberries inside. Some family traditions—like the delicious Thanksgiving dinner they'd just eaten—he'd gladly participate in.

But that didn't mean he was ready to get all overjoyed about Christmas. Not when it was filled with reminders of his failed marriage.

But he dutifully put on his jacket and piled into the car with his parents and grandmother. Brad and Mel had spent Thanksgiving with Mel's family, and Luke tried not to wish he'd been there. Tried not to wonder if Madison had missed him the way he'd missed her.

Right, he snorted at himself. *Keep dreaming.*

But that was the problem. He couldn't stop dreaming about the possibilities. He'd almost gone so far as to ask her out the other night at Brad and Mel's engagement party, until they'd been interrupted. And then he'd nearly called her half a dozen times this week. But every time he was about to, he remembered her reaction when they were teenagers and he'd told her he wanted to be a mechanic. He'd already had one wife who didn't respect what he did for a living. He certainly didn't need another.

She could have changed.

The thought had occurred to him more than once—and he had to admit she did seem different. She'd asked questions about his shop and seemed genuinely interested in his answers. But that didn't mean she'd want to date him.

"Oh, there are the Monroes and Brad." Dad honked his horn lightly as he pulled into the parking lot at Founder's Park, and the whole group turned toward them. Luke thought they all waved, but he wasn't positive, as his eyes went straight to Madison. She was bundled in a puffy white jacket, her face wreathed in a smile that Luke could almost convince himself was directed at him.

A smile grabbed his lips too as the Monroes waited for Dad to park the car. Luke got out and opened the door for his grandmother. Then the four of them made their way to the waiting group. After a few minutes of general chatter, they turned to follow the crowds heading toward the center of the park. Madison's parents went first, Mom fell in next to Brad and Mel, and Dad took Grandma's arm.

Madison and Luke were the only ones left. She gave him an uncertain smile.

"Shall we?" He gestured for her to follow his family, then fell into step next to her.

"Did you have a nice Thanksgiving?" Madison asked.

"Uh, yeah. It was nice. Thanks for taking Brad off our hands for a while."

She laughed, hitting his arm. "At least we got the brother with all the charm."

"Ouch. That was—"

But she grabbed his arm and pointed toward the center of the park. "I think that's the biggest tree they've ever had. Isn't it amazing?"

Luke tried to answer, but he couldn't think with her hand on him.

"Oh sorry." Madison let go. "I forgot you hate Christmas."

"I don't *hate* it," he muttered.

"Did dressing up as Santa change your mind?" she teased.

Luke snorted. "That definitely goes in the bad Christmas memories column."

Out of the corner of his eye, he saw her head turn toward him. "You have a whole column of bad Christmas memories?"

He stared at the back of his father's head a few feet in front of them. "The last few years? Yeah."

She was silent, and he could tell she was waiting for more. He appreciated that she didn't ask.

"But you have a good Christmas memories column too, right?" she finally said.

He let himself glance at her. She seemed to be concentrating on the back of his grandmother's feet.

"Yeah," he said. "I do."

She looked up, her smile overtaking him. "Good. Then we'll just have to make sure to add to that column this year."

"Hmm." So far the chances of that looked pretty good.

As they reached the tree, the rest of the group moved to the left. Madison started to follow, but Luke suddenly wanted her to himself.

"Come on." He grabbed her hand. "There's a better spot over here."

Madison didn't protest as he pulled her along, not stopping until they reached a nearly front-row spot.

"Wow. This is perfect." Madison's cheeks glowed and her breath puffed in front of her. "Good eye."

"I know." He suddenly realized he was still holding her hand and released his grip.

She lifted her fingers to her mouth and blew on them. "I heard there was a super cold front moving in, but I didn't think it was supposed to hit until tomorrow. I should have brought my gloves."

"Here." Luke held out a hand, palm up.

Madison blinked at it, then slowly placed her hand into it.

"Other one too." Luke waited for her to comply, then closed his other hand over the top of hers, making a cocoon. He concentrated on rubbing his hands back and forth over hers, not quite ready to meet her eyes.

"Warmer?" he asked after a moment.

"Much." Madison started to tug her hands away, but he tightened his around them.

"You'll get cold again," he warned.

"Good point." Her hands stilled in his, and he let his eyes come to hers. She was looking at him with—he wasn't quite sure what. But he did know it made him want to go through with his plan to ask her out.

"Welcome, ladies and gentlemen, boys and girls," a voice boomed over the loudspeaker.

Madison's eyes went to the small platform in front of the tree, where the town's mayor stood. "We have been lighting this tree in Founder's Park for nearly one hundred years. Tonight the honor will be done by Tabitha Carruth."

A young girl joined him on the platform, and Luke nudged Madison. "That's the girl who hugged me."

Madison smiled and nodded as she joined the whole town in the countdown.

In spite of himself, Luke joined in too, and when they got to zero, instead of watching the tree, he watched Madison's face, smiling as her anticipation turned to joy. She pulled her hands out from his to clap.

He turned to the tree then, joining in the applause as he took in the festive lights stretching skyward. It reminded him of when he was little and Christmas was filled with so much hope and promise.

He glanced at Madison, who was still clapping and cheering.

Maybe it could be again someday.

"There you two are." Melanie squeezed between them. "We've been looking all over. It's freezing out here. Everyone's waiting for y'all so we can leave."

"Sorry," Luke murmured. Now that she mentioned it, the temperature did seem to have dropped even more in the last few minutes, though Luke was still plenty warm from holding Madison's hands.

Melanie speed-marched them to the parking lot, then practically stuffed Madison into her parents' car.

"Goodnight," Luke called, just as Mel shut the door on her.

He couldn't hear Madison's answer. But she did wave to him.

He opened the back door of his parents' car and dropped inside.

"There," Mom said from next to him. "Now was that so bad?"

"It was fine," Luke conceded. But in his head, he added a little check mark to the good Christmas memories column.

Chapter 11

Madison rubbed at her temples. She was never going to be able to memorize all the components of the autonomic nervous system in horses.

Her phone dinged with a notification, and she told herself to ignore it. She could check her messages later. *After* she finished studying.

But she was *never* going to be done studying.

And it could be Tamara. They'd been texting back and forth all morning about how hard this exam was going to be.

She picked up the phone.

But it wasn't Tamara.

Luke's name stared at her, and her heart thumped a little harder. Which wasn't good.

She'd spent all day yesterday half expecting him to call. When he hadn't, she'd had to acknowledge that she'd read more into his holding her hands at the tree lighting ceremony than she should have. Again.

But she was over that.

Whatever he was texting about, it could wait.

She set the phone down and turned back to her book.

Her phone dinged again, and she ignored it, along with two more dings after that. By the fifth ding, she couldn't take it anymore. She had to at least turn off her notifications.

But instead of pressing the button to silence the phone, her finger tapped on the string of messages.

Look outside.

Hello? Madison?

I know you're there.

Seriously, have you looked outside?

You leave me no choice.

Madison stared at the last line. She left him no choice but to what?

In spite of her resolve to finish studying, her fingers started tapping out a reply.

But before she could finish it, her door buzzed.

She sighed. Just what she needed—one more distraction.

She kept tapping on her way to the door and hit send before she pressed the button on the intercom.

"Hello?"

There was no answer.

"Hello?" She didn't hide her impatience. She had things to do.

The speaker crackled to life. "Sorry. I was replying to your text."

"Luke?" She blinked at the intercom. "What are you doing here?"

"Did you even look outside?"

"No. I've been trying to—"

"Look outside. Now." The urgency in his voice sent her scurrying to the living room window that looked out over the parking lot. She hadn't opened the curtains this morning since it was supposed to be another unusually cold day, and she wanted to conserve as much heat as possible.

But she pulled them back now and gasped, then laughed. A thin layer of white covered everything, and big, fat flakes drifted through the air. Someone stood in the middle of the apartment's walkway, waving at her, and Madison laughed harder. Luke was all bundled up in a jacket, a red hat, and bright red gloves.

He gestured toward the front door as if indicating she should let him in, and she hurried back to the intercom to hit the unlock button.

She opened her apartment door, wrapping her arms around herself as a cold draft followed Luke into the building.

"What are you doing here?" she asked as she ushered him into her apartment so they could get out of the cold.

"It's snowing," he proclaimed, holding out his mittens to display the rapidly melting flakes.

Madison poked at one. "I see that. But I'm not sure it answers my question."

"Of course it does." Luke pulled off his hat, and his tousled hair fell over his forehead. "We're going sledding."

"Who's going sledding?"

"We are," Luke said, enunciating slowly. "You and me."

"I can't." She gazed toward the window, the fresh snow beckoning. But she had her priorities. "I have to study."

"Oh, come on," Luke wheedled, looking boyish and hopeful. "When's the last time it snowed before Christmas in River Falls? This is a once-in-a-lifetime opportunity."

Madison snorted. "No, it's not. It snowed the year—" She cut herself off before the words *we kissed* came out of her mouth. "So that's at least twice in a lifetime."

"Exactly. That's why we need to go today. For old times' sake."

Madison bit her lip. That did sound like a good reason to go.

But no. She had to study. She wasn't a kid who could just go sledding on a whim anymore. "I'm sorry. I really can't." She stepped toward the door to show him out.

"Please." He folded his hands in front of him. "Brad's working and my friend Mitch refuses to go and I don't really know anyone else well enough to ask."

"So go by yourself."

"Yeah, because that wouldn't be creepy at all. A thirty-year-old guy shows up at the sledding hill alone."

"You're thirty?" Sometimes Madison forgot he was nearly three years older than she was.

He rolled his eyes. "Not the point. But yes. My birthday was earlier this week and you missed it." His eyes lit up. "So this can be your present to me."

She shook her head with a laugh. "Since when do I get you a birthday present?"

"Since now. Come on. You know you want to. I can see it in your eyes."

She looked away so he wouldn't see how right he was. "What I want to do is get back to studying. I know it may be hard for you to believe, but I'm not some little kid. I have responsibilities and I take them seriously and I can't just—"

"That's not hard for me to believe." Luke stepped closer, and her gaze went to his face even though she didn't want it to. He looked serious. Earnest. "I know you take your education seriously. But I also know you work really hard and need a break sometimes." He tilted his head, giving her a wide-eyed puppy-dog stare. "Just for an hour? I'll help you study when we get back. Plus, I'll count it as another two-fifths of your payback for my Santa performance."

Madison pressed her lips together to avoid saying yes. But her head seemed to be bobbing up and down.

"Yes!" Luke punched a fist into the air. "Okay, go get bundled up. It's pretty cold out."

Madison moved to the coat closet in the hallway without a word.

This was a bad idea.

A really bad idea.

And yet, she couldn't help feeling a little giddy as she pulled on her boots and coat and hat and gloves.

This was a bad idea she was really looking forward to.

Chapter 12

"How about over there?" Luke pointed to a spot at the far end of the sledding hill, away from the masses of laughing children.

"What about all the trees?" Madison held the plastic sled over her heart like a shield.

"There are like three trees," he pointed out. "We'll just steer around them. Come on." He carried a plastic sled just like hers but also dragged a classic wooden toboggan behind him.

"If I crash, it's your fault." Madison walked next to him as they passed parents standing at the top of the hill watching their kids sled—a few brave parents joining in the fun.

Luke had a sudden flash of himself and Madison sitting on the toboggan with a kid smooshed between them.

He sped up his walk, letting her fall slightly behind. But the image stayed right with him.

He led them a little farther, into the untracked snow, then stopped. "Do you want to go first or should I?"

"This was your idea. You're going first." Madison's cheeks and nose glowed red in the cold, but she looked happy. Or at least not upset.

"I was hoping you'd say that." He grinned and let go of the toboggan rope, dropping the plastic sled in front of him and plopping onto it on his stomach to ride down penguin-style.

For a moment, he heard Madison's laugh, and then the only sound was the whooshing of the snow under the sled. Powder flew up around him, coating his face and the back of his neck, and he gave a loud whoop, steering between two trees. He hadn't felt this young and carefree in a long time.

When the sled finally slowed to a stop, he rolled off it and lay staring up at the sky for a moment. The snowfall had lightened to scattered flurries, and he tracked the progress of a flake before catching it and watching it melt.

Then he jumped to his feet and waved his arm over his head to coax Madison down the hill.

She didn't move for a minute, so he waved again, calling, "Come on. It's fun."

Slowly, she set her sled at the top of the track he'd cut, then lowered herself gingerly onto it.

She dragged her hands on the ground as the sled started down the hill. But after a few feet, she lifted them, and the sled picked up speed. She let out a squeal that might have been fear or might have been joy. But as she got closer, Luke could see the smile on her face, and he smiled too.

The sled came to a stop at his feet, and he held out a hand to help her up.

"That was—"

"Fun, right?" He bent down to pick up her sled.

"I was going to say crazy," she gasped out. "But yeah, kind of fun too."

"Well, come on. Let's do it again." They started up the hill side by side, but the fresh snow was slick, and Madison flailed. Luke caught her arm just in time to keep her from toppling, but then his feet tried to kick out from under him. Madison tightened her grip, keeping him upright, and they skidded the rest of the way up the hill like that.

They each took several more runs down the hill, Luke alternating between the plastic sled and the toboggan but Madison sticking with her plastic sled. Fortunately, the path uphill was much easier once they'd made boot prints in the snow. Unfortunately, that meant Luke didn't have an excuse to hold her hand anymore.

"Is it getting dark out?" Madison asked after a while. "What time is it?"

Luke shrugged. He didn't know what time it was, and he didn't care. He'd gladly stay out here all night. But Madison pulled out her phone. "Five o'clock! I really have to get home."

"One more run," Luke implored. "You haven't tried the toboggan yet."

"And I'm not going to. I told you, that thing is a death trap."

"It's not a death trap." Luke lined up the toboggan at the top of the hill. "Come on. We'll go down together. Just once. And then we can go."

Madison eyed the toboggan and then him. "You're not going to give up until I say yes, are you?"

"Nope." He gestured to the sled. "All aboard."

She sighed and rolled her eyes but moved closer.

He squatted to hold the sled in place. "You take the front."

"But then I have to steer."

"There's already a track. There's nothing to steer." And also, if he sat behind her, he'd have an excuse to wrap his arms around her. He chose not to say that part out loud.

"Fine." She sat at the front of the toboggan, gathering the rope into her hands. He waited until she was settled, then climbed on behind her, sticking a leg on each side of her. He kept his hands planted in the snow so the sled wouldn't start down the hill before they were ready.

"You know how to steer this thing, right?" He leaned forward, letting her vanilla and cinnamon scent drift over him.

"What?" She turned her head, and they were face-to-face, inches apart. "You said I wouldn't have to steer." Her eyes sprang wide with panic.

"Relax." His gaze fell on her lips, only inches from his own. "You probably won't. But just in case, pull left on the rope to go left, right to go right."

"Left left. Right right. I guess I can handle that." Madison licked her lips.

"Okay, then. Get ready." He had to get this sled moving or he might just kiss those lips. "Set. Go."

He pushed off with his hands, then wrapped them around her waist as the sled took off.

Madison whipped her head to the front with a soft shriek, and then they were picking up speed.

Luke let himself hold her tighter.

Madison shifted, and the sled veered off the track.

"Go right," he called.

But the sled cut farther to the left, straight toward a large pine tree.

"Other right," he yelled.

Madison pulled the rope to the other side, and the sled corrected slightly, but it wasn't enough.

The tree was only forty feet away and closing fast.

"Bail out," Luke called.

"What?" Madison jerked but didn't get off the sled.

Thirty feet.

"We have to get off," he called again.

Still she didn't move.

Luke cinched his arms around her, pulling her tight to his chest, then gave a hard jerk to the side, rolling them into the snow, trying to cushion her with his body. But they had too much momentum, and he rolled a couple of times, losing his grip on her in the process.

The moment he stopped, he pushed himself upright. "Madison?"

She was only a couple feet from him, lying on her back with both hands over her left eye.

"Madison?" He scrambled through the snow and dropped to his knees at her side. "Are you all right?"

She groaned but nodded. "I think so. My eye . . ."

Gently, he wrapped his hands around hers and pulled them away from her face.

He couldn't hold back a gasp at the bruise already forming there.

"What?" Madison tried to cover her eye again, but Luke stilled her hand.

He scooped up a gloveful of snow, gently laying it against the bruise. "Looks like you're going to have a bit of a shiner. I'm so sorry. I must have hit you when I lost my grip."

Madison sat up cautiously, most of the snow falling off her face. "Well, on the bright side, at least we didn't hit the tree." She pointed to the toboggan which had rammed itself against the trunk only fifteen feet away. "That probably would have hurt worse."

"I'm sorry." He tried not to imagine her slamming into the tree face-first. It was all his fault. "I shouldn't have talked you into going down on the toboggan. I really didn't think we'd get off the track."

Madison shook her head. "I probably should have mentioned that I tend to get my left and right mixed up."

Luke chuckled. "That might have been good to know. Come on, let's get you home and get some ice on that." He got to his feet, then helped her up and went to fetch the toboggan. When they reached the top of the hill, he insisted on taking all three sleds.

Most of the families had cleared out by now, and the sun had lowered enough that the lights over the hill had come on, illuminating the softly falling snow. It would have been romantic—if he hadn't just accidentally given her a black eye.

When they got back to her apartment building, he jumped out to walk her to the door. She unlocked it and stepped inside.

"So, I guess I'll—uh—see you around." He toed the threshold.

Madison looked at him over her shoulder, narrowing her good eye but then wincing and covering the puffy one. "Where do you think you're going? You said you'd help me study if I went sledding."

"I just figured— You still want me to?"

"Yes. I mean, unless you don't want to?" She peered at him with one eye.

"I want to." Luke stepped decisively into the building and followed her into her apartment. They peeled off their winter gear and piled it on the small dining room table near the door. "First, some ice for your eye."

The apartment was small—definitely not the luxury condo he would have pictured her in—and he strode the few feet into the kitchen, pulling open the freezer. It was nearly empty, aside from a bag of frozen strawberries and a package of chicken.

"You don't have ice," he called.

"I don't really use it for anything." Madison's voice trailed away, and he looked over his shoulder. She'd moved into the living room and lowered herself to the couch.

"Do you have any ice cube trays?"

"Somewhere. Maybe in the cupboard above the fridge? Don't worry about it. I'm fine."

"You're not fine." He reached into the cupboard and pulled down the ice cube trays, filling them and sticking them in the freezer. Then he grabbed the bag of strawberries.

"This will have to do for now." He brought it to her. "You should have ice in a few hours."

"Those are for my smoothies." Madison gave the strawberries a skeptical look but took the bag. She lifted it to her eye but pulled it away with a yelp.

"I know it hurts now, but trust me, it will help. One second." He returned to the kitchen and rummaged through drawers until he found a towel. He hurried back to her side and took the bag from her hand, wrapping it in the towel. Then he squatted in front of her and gently brought the bag to her eye. When she winced, he brought his other hand to her opposite cheek. "Trust me, it will help," he repeated.

She nodded, lifting her hand to hold the bag in place.

Right. He should let go.

He pulled both hands back and stood. "Maybe we should call Mel or Brad to take a look at it."

Madison shook her head. "I'm fine. Really. Now sit. Quiz me." She gestured to a thick black textbook. "Chapter 26. There are self-study questions on page 346."

Luke obediently sat, flipped the book open, and started quizzing her. He barely understood a single question he read, but he sure did love listening to her responses. Whenever she was confident about an answer, she would reply with such a smile that he wanted to just keep asking the same question over and over. But then, when she was less certain, she'd give him a look of such hope that he had to remind himself not to misinterpret it.

When they'd finally come to the end of the questions, Luke closed the book reluctantly. "You're ready for this," he announced.

"I sure hope so." Madison pulled the bag of strawberries off her eye. "I think they're starting to thaw."

Luke took the bag from her, brushing a finger delicately beneath the bruise. "I think it helped."

"Oh. That's good," Madison whispered, and he suddenly realized how close he was to her.

He stood abruptly and sped to the kitchen, shoving the berries back into the freezer. The frigid air felt good on his suddenly too-hot face. He grabbed the ice cube tray. "The ice should be done soon," he called.

And then he ran out of things to do in the freezer. He closed it and shuffled awkwardly back to the living room. "So, um, I guess I should go. Unless you have more studying you need me to . . ."

"Oh. Uh. No. I've taken up enough of your time already." Madison stood. "I'm sure you have better things to do. But thanks for your help."

Luke nodded. *You don't have better things to do*, his heart screamed.

"Anytime." He pulled on his jacket. "And thanks for sledding with me."

"It was fun." The left side of Madison's cheek didn't move with her smile.

"Aside from the black eye." Luke stepped closer to her as he pulled on his hat. "I really am sorry."

"I know you are. And I forgive you."

"Good." Luke's eyes traveled from her shiner to her lips. What would happen if—

"Luke?"

"Yeah?" His gaze lifted back to her eyes.

"Will you be at church tomorrow?"

"Oh." He hadn't expected that question. It'd been a long time since he'd been to church. Growing up, he'd gone because there hadn't been a choice. It was what his family had done. And he did believe in God. He'd kept going for a while after he'd left home, but Cindy really wasn't a churchgoer, and after a shorter time than he'd like to admit, he'd fallen out of the habit.

But now, the thought of going to church felt oddly compelling. And he didn't think it was only because Madison was the one asking him. Although that didn't hurt.

"You know what," he finally answered. "I just might be there."

Chapter 13

Madison pulled the thick faux-fur-lined hood up over her head as she got out of her car in Beautiful Savior's parking lot. Thanks to the ice Luke had made, her eye wasn't nearly as puffy as it had been yesterday, but it was an ugly shade of black and purple. And way too painful to even attempt covering with makeup.

She scanned the parking lot, trying not to be disappointed when she didn't spot Luke's truck.

He'd said he *might be* here, she reminded herself. It wasn't his fault if she'd chosen to interpret that as a *yes*.

She walked toward the church, reprimanding herself for getting so wrapped up in this guy. So he'd dragged her sledding and taken care of her after she'd gotten hurt and quizzed her on horse physiology. That didn't mean he liked her—at least not *seriously* liked her. She was just a diversion for him—the same way she had been when they were kids. And she'd be stupid to read more into it than that.

Keeping her head ducked low, she stepped onto the sidewalk that led to the church's front doors. Some of yesterday's snow had already melted, but clumps still clung to the bushes alongside the building, giving it a magical feel. Sledding yesterday had been the most fun she'd had in a long time, black eye and all.

Maybe Luke was right. Maybe she did need to take a break like that once in a while. In fact, maybe she'd go to the downtown Christmas market after church. She could always look for a wedding gift for Brad and Mel there.

She entered the church, pushing her hood off in the sudden wave of heat.

"Oh my goodness, Madison. What happened to you?" Ava pulled Joseph toward her as Madison realized too late that she should have waited until she was seated to take off the hood.

"It's nothing, really." Madison waved them off. "Luke came over yesterday and—"

"He did this to you?" Joseph's jaw hardened, and he looked over his shoulder. "Zeb, come here."

"What? No!" Madison shook her head so hard that she could feel the blood pulse in her bruised eye. But she couldn't let them think that. "We went sledding, and I steered us right toward a tree. You know how I get left and right mixed up."

Ava's eyes widened. "You hit a tree?"

Madison shook her head again. This was why she wasn't a storyteller. "Luke pulled us off the sled just in time. But somehow in the process I hit my eye on something. It could have been a lot worse though."

"Wow." Ava squeezed her arm. "Sounds like you have your own superhero."

"It's not like that," Madison mumbled.

"Mmm hmm." Ava grinned. "Want to sit with us?"

Madison scanned the nearly empty lobby. "Thanks, but I'm going to stick near the back. Fewer people asking questions that way." And maybe a chance to catch Luke if he did show up.

"I understand." Ava smiled, her scars pinching at the left side of her face, and Madison thought again of how brave she was. Of course, it had largely been Joseph's unrelenting love that had coaxed Ava to really live again after her accident.

Madison wondered sometimes what it would be like to love someone like that. Or be loved like that.

"Try to stay in one piece," Joseph said as Ava pulled him away. "I want you to assist with surgeries on Tuesday."

"Really?" Madison gasped. Joseph had said before that she'd be ready soon, but he'd never put a date to it.

"Really." He grinned and followed his wife into the church.

Madison entered behind them, dropping into an open spot in the back pew. She let herself take one more look around, just to make sure she hadn't missed Luke, then closed her eyes to pray.

Church bells rang out over Beautiful Savior's parking lot as Luke threw his truck into park. He jumped out and jogged toward the big brick church, relieved to see he wasn't the only one who was late, as a frazzled looking young couple across the lot appeared to be trying to wrangle their crew—one of whom was crying and another of whom kept stopping to pick up handfuls of dirty snow.

At least they had an excuse for being late. His only excuse was indecisiveness. As much as he wanted to see Madison, he'd nearly talked himself out of coming for exactly that reason—he was getting dangerously close to falling for her. But in the end, he'd decided that he needed to at least see how her eye was doing.

So here he was, pulling open the church door.

He nodded to the greeter who smiled at him, then made his way to the sanctuary as the congregation began to sing the first hymn. He spotted Madison instantly, right at the back.

Perfect.

He stepped over to her pew, leaning down to whisper, "Is this seat taken?"

She jumped but looked up with a smile, the black and purple of her eye doing nothing to diminish her beauty. She slid over and angled her hymnal toward him.

"How's your eye?" He leaned closer to whisper, her vanilla scent cloaking him.

"Better," she murmured. "Doesn't hurt as much."

"Good." He turned to the hymnal and let his voice join with hers, feeling strangely comfortable as he settled into his seat.

After a moment, he took the hymnal from her and held it for both of them, and she glanced at him with a soft smile.

He smiled back but then directed his eyes to the page. He couldn't let himself go feeling all these content, comfortable feelings with her.

As the hymn ended and Pastor Calvano began the readings, Luke angled his body away from her. But he had to turn his head if he wanted to see Pastor Calvano, and Madison was right there in his peripheral vision.

It was a relief when Pastor Calvano finally climbed into the pulpit to deliver his sermon, since it forced Luke to shift his gaze to the right, away from Madison. Now he couldn't see her out of his peripheral vision.

Even when he tried.

"I don't know about y'all, but the Christmas season is my favorite time of year," Pastor Calvano began. Luke crossed his arms in front of him. His memories of the past few Christmases spoiled the whole season for him. But then he thought of Madison's comment about adding more checks to the good Christmas memories column. Maybe this year he'd be able to do that.

"The Christmas lights, the presents, the food . . ." Pastor Calvano patted his middle. "Oh, the food." The congregation chuckled, and next to him, Luke heard Madison's sweet, low laugh. It sent a ripple through him that he forced himself to ignore.

"But to me, the best part is the anticipation," Pastor Calvano continued. "The anticipation of celebrating Jesus' birth, of course. But I admit that when I was a kid, what I really anticipated was what would be under the tree. I'd see those wrapped gifts, and I'd let my imagination run away from me. That one had to be the skateboard I'd asked for. And that one was the

Astroray Gun I'd seen advertised on TV. And don't forget the gyroscope. I really wanted one of those. And a lot of the time, I was right. My parents had taken my not-so-subtle hints and gotten me what I wanted."

Pastor Calvano leaned forward on the pulpit. "And then there was the year I wanted a horse. I just knew my parents were going to get one for me. I knew they couldn't put it under the tree, of course. But I'd played out the whole scene in my imagination a thousand times. We'd open all the gifts under the tree, my parents would pretend there was nothing else, then they'd say we should go for a drive. They'd take me to the stables, where they'd present me with my very own horse. And then we'd bring it home. To our house in the middle of Memphis." He paused as the congregation laughed. Luke laughed along, remembering suddenly how much he'd always enjoyed Pastor Calvano's anecdotes—they always made God's Word so real and relatable.

"Y'all." Pastor Calvano cut into the laughter. "It didn't happen. That carefully crafted scene my imagination had conjured was just that: imaginary. I never admitted it to my mama and daddy, but I was disappointed. Don't get me wrong—they gave me a lot of nice gifts that year. But still, that Christmas didn't live up to what I'd imagined." Pastor Calvano paused, letting his gaze travel the room, and Luke could tell he was about to switch gears.

Next to him, Madison shifted, and Luke didn't have the willpower not to look at her. She was leaning forward, her hand on the pew between them. It would be so easy to rest his own hand there too.

Instead, he folded his hands in his lap and angled himself nearly sideways so she disappeared from his vision again.

"I was thinking about that very first Christmas," Pastor Calvano continued. "About the anticipation. God had foretold it from that very first sin in the Garden of Eden. But not many people knew it was coming when it did. Aside from Mary and Joseph. Can you imagine their anticipation? Imagine what they thought it'd be like. Picture Mary bustling around her house, preparing for her new arrival. Joseph, lovingly crafting a fine cradle. They must have thought it was all going to be perfect. After all, this was God's Son they were preparing for. It *had* to be perfect."

He paused, and Luke found himself leaning forward, his own anticipation growing.

"But then, just when they should be finishing their preparations, they had to make the trek to Bethlehem for the census. And when they got there, there was nowhere for them to stay. The best anyone could offer them was a spot in a stable with the animals. And as if sleeping in a stable while pregnant wasn't bad enough, little baby Jesus decided he wasn't going to wait any longer to be born. Mary gave birth right there in the stable. To the Son of God."

Pastor Calvano shook his head. "All their preparations, everything they imagined this day would be, went out the window. They placed Jesus in a manger instead of a cradle. It must have felt anything but perfect."

Pastor Calvano scanned the congregation. "I don't know about y'all, but if I were Mary and Joseph, I'd be thinking that surely God must have messed up. This wasn't how things were supposed to go. It wasn't how they'd imagined it. Surely, God could have arranged for the census to take place at another time. Or for Jesus to be born after they'd returned home. Or for a thousand different scenarios to ensure that the King of the World wouldn't have to be born in a barn."

Pastor Calvano picked up his Bible. "It's true. God *could* have. But here's what he tells us about why Jesus was born when he was: 'When the time had fully come, God sent his Son, born of a woman, born under law, to redeem those under law.'"

He set the Bible down, gazing out at the congregation thoughtfully. "'When the time had fully come.' Who do you suppose determined when that time was?" He paused only a beat. "God. God determined when the time was right for Jesus to be born. To Mary and Joseph, it may have seemed like a mistake. It may not have lived up to what they'd imagined.

But this was God's plan." Pastor Calvano emphasized each word of the sentence.

"Everything was exactly as it should be. In fact, it wasn't that God had failed to live up to what they'd imagined. It was that they'd failed to imagine what God could do. They couldn't grasp the greatness, the fullness, the depth of God's plan of salvation. It was a plan that only God could come up with. A plan no human could have imagined. It was a plan from a God who, as Paul says in Ephesians, 'is able to do immeasurably more than all we ask or imagine.' That's what he did on the first Christmas, sending his Son into the world to live and die for us. He exceeded the limits of even the wildest human imagination."

Luke relaxed a little into the pew, accidentally turning toward Madison. She glanced at him with a smile, and he felt his own lips lift. He was glad he'd come. Not just to be with Madison. But because he'd needed to be reminded of this message that had been pushed to the back of his mind—and his heart—for so long.

"And that's what he does today," Pastor Calvano continued. "Immeasurably more than all we ask or imagine." He paused. "Now, maybe you don't think so. Maybe you don't feel like your life has lived up to your imagination, let alone exceeded it."

Luke barely resisted laughing out loud. His life wasn't even close to what he'd imagined. Divorced. No children. Not even a dog.

Next to him, Madison was nodding—and so were heads all around the church.

Luke let out a breath. Maybe he wasn't the only one wondering how his life had become such a mess.

"The thing is," Pastor Calvano continued. "God created this world to be perfect. We should be living here in bliss, with no problems in sight." He shook his head with an ironic laugh. "Oh, how far we've fallen. With the first sin, that was all destroyed. The world was no longer as it should be. Now there was pain. There were problems. There was death." Pastor

Calvano shook his head. "This doesn't sound like a very good sermon for the Christmas season, does it?"

Madison's soft laugh caught Luke's attention, and he turned toward her again. She scooted a little closer to him, and he turned back to the pulpit, trying not to be aware of her presence.

"But it is," Pastor Calvano continued. "It's the most Christmassy sermon I could give. Because in order to understand the meaning of that first Christmas, we have to go back to the beginning and understand *why* we needed it. Why God came up with this unimaginable plan to send his Son into the world. It wasn't so we could hang up Christmas lights or so we could exchange gifts or even so we could eat all that delicious food. It was to *save us from our sins.* It was to make everything as it should be again. To give us the promise that though things in this world are all messed up, God has given us exactly what we need at exactly the right time. He sent his Son when the time had fully come. And when he knows the time is right, he will bring us to be with him in heaven. And as joyous as our Christmas celebrations are here on earth—nothing can compare to the joy we will experience there. It will be so much more than we could ever ask or imagine. To him be all glory. Amen."

Luke stood with the rest of the congregation, his heart filling as they sang "O Come, O Come, Emmanuel." It'd been a long time since he'd thought about the real meaning of Christmas, and for the first time in years, the joy of that meaning felt like something worth holding on to.

Chapter 14

Peace washed over Madison as the service ended. Her life may not be what she'd imagined—although she'd never really known *what* to imagine about her life—but it was good. A gift from God. She had a job she loved, her own apartment, school, and— Her eyes shifted to the right. Luke was still watching the front of the church, but his thoughts seemed to be somewhere else.

She hoped the service had been as uplifting for him as it had been for her.

People started filing past them out the church doors. Madison didn't miss the knowing grin Ava sent her way as the Calvanos trooped past.

"Make sure you put some ice on that," Joseph said as he passed them.

"I will," Madison called.

Luke's head jerked up, and he seemed to realize at last that the service was over. "Sorry." He stood. "Guess I was lost in thought."

"I figured," Madison said easily. "I planned to poke you if you were still thinking when Pastor Calvano wanted to leave."

Luke laughed. "That's very kind of you."

"I know." She followed him out of the pew and into the lobby, where several groups stood chatting.

"Hey." Luke turned to her. "Thanks for inviting me. I'm glad I came."

"Me too."

"Are you headed home, or do you need to . . ." He circled a hand at the mingling crowds.

Madison bit her lip, thinking of her earlier plan to go to the Christmas market. It would probably be boring on her own. "Did you find a gift for Brad and Mel yet? From the wedding party?"

Luke looked confused, as if he didn't follow the conversation, but he shook his head. "Not yet. But don't worry, I will."

"Do you want some help?" Madison asked quickly, before she could change her mind.

"What? You decided you don't want me to get one hundred percent credit for the gift?" Luke teased.

"Exactly." Madison grinned, grateful he was keeping things lighthearted. "There's a Christmas market downtown today. I thought maybe we'd find something there."

Luke's lips lifted into a smile. "Let's do it."

They marched toward the door.

"You realize this counts for another one-fifth of my payback, right?" Madison asked as they stepped outside. Her foot slid across a patch of ice, nearly sending her onto her back, but Luke caught her arm.

"Careful. It's slippery with everything melting." He slid his hand into hers and held on tight as they continued into the parking lot. "Anyway, I'm doing you a favor coming shopping with you, so this does not count as payback."

"No. I'm doing you a favor," Madison argued. "You're the one who's supposed to get them a gift."

"Ah, but since I'm the one owed the debt, I get to decide what counts."

Madison laughed but gave in. "Can't compete with that logic."

"Good. Now, my car or yours?"

"Maybe yours? Mine has been making a weird sound."

"What kind of sound?" Luke asked, shifting his grip as they reached an icy spot.

"Like a plink, plink, plink." Madison tried to replicate the sound. "Or no, more of a cha-cha, cha-chang."

But Luke was laughing. "How was that again?"

She shoved his arm. "Oh, I don't know how to describe it."

"No, you did a great job. I can just picture your car dancing." He was still laughing.

"You know what, never mind. I'm not going to help you shop."

"Okay, okay. I'm sorry." He was still chuckling. "Why don't you bring it by the shop? I'll take a look at it." He let go of her hand to open the passenger door of his truck. Madison slid into the seat, making herself take a long, steadying breath as he rounded to the driver's side.

He hadn't been *holding her hand*. He'd been keeping her from falling.

And this wasn't a date. It was a shopping trip. Completely utilitarian.

Whatever was going on here, she was not going to make the mistake of thinking he was interested in her again. She wasn't a silly fifteen-year-old anymore. She was a grown woman. A grown woman who didn't get crushes.

Luke opened his truck door, and every word of the lecture she'd just given herself jumped overboard.

"So—" Luke started the truck and kept both hands on the wheel as he headed the few blocks to the downtown area. "Where should we park?"

"You can park in the clinic parking lot," Madison said. "The streets beyond it are closed for the market. Joseph won't mind."

"As long as Joseph won't mind," Luke muttered, but he turned into the driveway and pulled into one of the few remaining spots.

"Wait there, in case it's slippery." He hopped out of the truck and jogged around to her side, opening her door and holding out a hand to help her down. Madison hesitated. It might be less risky to take her chances with the ice. But Luke reached forward and grabbed her arm. "Don't fall," he warned. "I feel bad enough about giving you a black eye."

"Don't say that." Madison let him help her down. "It wasn't your fault. I should have been smart enough to bail when you told me to."

"And I shouldn't have pressured you into sitting in front."

"And I should be able to tell my right from my left."

"And I should have—"

"Tell you what," Madison interrupted. "How about we split the blame fifty-fifty. Now, come on. We have a mission."

"Yes, ma'am." Luke tightened his grip on her hand and led them into the crowds surging toward downtown, where craft booths and food trucks filled the blocked-off streets. "Any chance this mission includes lunch? I'm famished."

Madison eyed him. Was he trying to turn this into a date? Or was he just hungry?

"There." He pointed toward a barbecue food truck stationed between the Book Den and Daisy's, before nearly dragging Madison off her feet to get to it. So, hungry then.

Good. It was good he didn't see this as a date.

Because it wasn't.

But when she pulled out her credit card, he shook his head. "This is on me."

Madison swallowed and put her card away. So it *was* a date?

She had no idea anymore—which was probably an issue, since she'd been the one to invite him in the first place.

He led the way to a cluster of tables that had been set up along the sidewalk, choosing one that felt way too small for two people, and set her food in front of her. Madison closed her eyes and bowed her head.

"Are you praying?" Luke asked softly.

She nodded, opening her eyes. "Does it bother you?"

"No." Luke swallowed. "I was just wondering if I could join you."

"Oh. Of course. Do you want me to— Or do you . . ." She wasn't always one hundred percent comfortable praying out loud—except when she was by herself—but for some reason the thought of praying with him didn't feel weird.

"I could try," Luke said, clearing his throat. "Although I'm afraid I might be a little rusty."

"That's okay." Impulsively, Madison reached across the table and grabbed his hands, slamming her eyelids shut before she could see his reaction.

His fingers closed around hers, and she sighed softly. This felt way too perfect.

"Lord," Luke began. "Thank you for the opportunity to worship you this morning. It has been way too long, but somehow you knew it was what I needed today. And you brought someone into my path to remind me of that at just the right time." His fingers squeezed Madison's for a second, and she caught her breath. Had God really used her to do that?

"Please bless our search for a gift for Brad and Mel," Luke continued. "And help Madison's eye to heal quickly." This time, she was the one to squeeze his hand. "And thank you for this meal," Luke added. "May it be as delicious as it smells. In Jesus' name. Amen."

Madison was still laughing as she opened her eyes and pulled her hands back.

"So?" Luke looked adorably uncertain. "Rusty?"

She shook her head. "Not in the least."

They dug into their meal, chatting about the changes to River Falls since Luke had left over a decade ago.

"What about the crossing guard? Mrs. Pike?" Luke asked. "She was always a fixture here."

"She died a few years ago," Madison answered. "Her son took over."

"I hope he's not as scary as she was."

"Luke!" Madison tossed her napkin at him.

"What? One time she caught me crossing before she'd blown her whistle, and she made me stand right there in the middle of the intersection and put on the vest and take her whistle and stop sign and pull crossing guard duty the rest of the morning. And when I didn't want to put her whistle in my mouth, she chewed me out. It was humiliating."

Madison's laugh had grown quietly as he'd told the story, but now she couldn't hold it back anymore. It exploded in a mortifying snort.

Luke blinked at her for a second, then his own laugh blasted out. People at nearby tables stared, but most were smiling.

When they'd finally gotten their giggles under control, Madison stood. "Come on. We need to get on with the mission."

"Yes, ma'am."

Luke grabbed their trash in one hand and wrapped the other around Madison's even though the temperature had warmed enough that she doubted there were any more patches of ice.

She decided not to point that out. Just in case there were some invisible ice patches.

They wandered from booth to booth, browsing everything from handcrafted wooden ornaments to cowboy hats that Luke insisted they try on. By the time they reached the end of the street an hour and a half later, they'd had plenty of laughs, a few conversations, and several . . . looks. But they still had no gift to show for their efforts.

"This is impossible," Madison whined—but she was pretty sure it wasn't as convincing as it could have been since she couldn't stop smiling.

"I know." Luke was smiling too. "Now what? Order something on-line?"

"There has to be . . ." Madison scanned the buildings. "There." She pointed down the street. "Let's try Henderson's."

"The art gallery?"

"Yeah. Unless you don't think—"

"I think it's genius. Come on." He cinched her hand closer, and they speed-walked into the art gallery.

Inside, they slowed and strolled past piece after piece. Abstract geometric shapes. Bucolic cow pastures. A Nashville cityscape.

"What about this one?" Madison stopped in front of a nighttime scene of a forest.

Luke frowned at it. "Too bleak."

Madison groaned and dropped her forehead onto his shoulder. It only made contact for a second before she jerked upright. What had she been thinking?

"This is impossible." That was what she'd been thinking. Every time she liked a piece, he didn't, and vice versa.

"We have half the store to go yet," Luke said, but he didn't sound hopeful. "Don't give up." He pulled her around the next corner, then stopped so abruptly that she ran into him.

"Ouch." She lifted her free hand to her bruised eye.

"Sorry." Luke spun to her. "Are you all right?"

"Yeah." She lowered her hand. "Why'd you stop?"

"Because I have a feeling we're about to agree on something." He gestured to the photographs on the wall in front of them.

"Oh wow. These are . . ." Madison stepped closer, and her eyes fell on the sign in the center of the wall. "No wonder. These are Ava's."

"They're really great." Luke pointed to a mountain skyline silhouetted against a starry sky.

"Yeah. They are." Madison moved toward a closeup of a rushing waterfall.

"What about this one?" Luke tugged her closer to him, his cedar and coffee scent beckoning her closer still.

She forced herself to focus on the photo—an overview of the entire River Falls valley bathed in a coppery sunset glow. "That's the one," she breathed.

"Really? We did it?" Luke grabbed both of her shoulders and dropped his forehead to hers. "I thought this moment would never come." His breath breezed over her, and all she could think was that they were close enough to—

He pulled back suddenly. "I'll go find someone to help us."

"Okay," Madison said weakly. She watched him go, then sagged against the wall.

Any hope she'd had of controlling this crush had just gone rushing right down the waterfall in Ava's picture.

But maybe that was okay. Because her feelings were starting to seem less and less one-sided.

Unless she was letting her imagination run away with her, the way Pastor Calvano had with his desire for a horse. She went back and forth, trying to weigh the evidence in her mind. But by the time Luke came striding back with Mr. Henderson, she was more confused than ever.

"That's a great choice," Mr. Henderson said when Luke pointed out the picture. "It will look lovely in your home."

"Oh no, it's not for us," Madison jumped in. "I mean, we're not— It's a gift. For my sister and his brother. They're getting married."

"Ah, a perfect wedding gift," Mr. Henderson said smoothly. He seemed unaware that he'd just sent Madison into never-before-heard-of levels of flustered.

Luke seemed to have noticed, though, judging by the way he was grinning at her.

She stuck her tongue out at him, then rolled her eyes at herself. What was she, two?

She followed as Luke and Mr. Henderson carried the framed picture to the front. Mr. Henderson rang up the purchase, and Madison had a heart-stopping moment when she realized she might have to put the whole thing on her credit card.

But Luke pulled out his card. "I'll pay for it and then collect the money from everyone."

"Are you sure?" Madison hated to ask that of him, but she didn't see any other solution. "I'll put a check in the mail tomorrow," she promised.

"Or you could just give it to me in person." Luke raised an eyebrow, and Madison wanted to ask when she was going to see him. But Mr. Henderson held out the receipt for Luke to sign.

Luke picked up the picture with both hands, leaving Madison's hand empty for the first time today—and she didn't like it. Maybe in the truck she'd find a way to subtly slip her hand back into his.

Luke fidgeted with the steering wheel, mostly so he wouldn't grab Madison's hand. But also because it was the only way to deal with the nerves surging through him right now.

Should he ask her out? Maybe kiss her when he dropped her off?

He was pretty sure she'd be okay with that. Pretty sure she might like him to, actually.

But if he was wrong . . .

"Do you think Brad and Mel will like the picture?" he asked, just for something to take his mind off kissing.

Madison laughed without sounding amused. "Your guess is as good as mine." She licked her lips, and Luke was back to thinking about kissing. "Mel and I aren't exactly close."

"No?" Luke didn't know if he considered himself close to his brother, but he'd always figured sisters would have a tighter bond. "Why not?"

"Oh, I don't know." Madison flopped her head back on the seat, pursing her lips in concentration.

Luke looked away so he could focus on her words, not her lips.

"She's always been the perfect child, you know?" Madison said. "She's known what she wanted to do since she came out of the womb, and she spent her whole life working for it, and now she has it. She's a doctor. She's about to get married. I'm sure she'll be a mom soon. It's like everything just fell into place for her."

Luke eyed her. "And that's a bad thing?"

"No." Madison sighed. "I sound like a horrible person right now, don't I?"

Luke chuckled. "Not horrible, no."

"I'm happy for her." Madison sat forward, rubbing at her temples. "I really am. And I'm happy with where my life is too. It's just . . . No one else seems to be."

"And do they need to be?" Luke asked.

Madison glanced at him, as if surprised by the question. "No. Yes. I don't know. I guess I'd like them to be. But I know as soon as they find out I graduated as a vet tech, they're going to be like, 'Oh, that's a nice little job, dear. Now when are you going to become a doctor like your sister?'"

Luke laughed. "That was a good impression of your mother. But I'm sure she'd never say that."

Madison shrugged. "Do your parents ever give you a hard time for being just a mechanic?"

Luke froze, his hands going rigid on the wheel. He'd been an idiot, thinking she'd stoop to going out with *just a mechanic.*

"Frankly, I don't care what my parents think about me being *just a mechanic.*" He ground out the words through his clenched teeth. "I like what I do, I'm good at it, and I don't have anything to prove to anyone." *Not even you,* he added silently.

"Luke, I didn't mean—"

"I know exactly what you meant." He pulled into the parking lot at Beautiful Savior. "You've made it clear plenty of times what you think of my career choice."

"I— What?" Madison looked confused and near tears, and Luke looked away so he wouldn't accidentally feel compassion for her.

He pulled up next to her car and waited for her to get out.

"Luke, I didn't even know what you did until a few weeks ago." She laid a hand on his arm. He flinched but didn't pull away. Nor did he look at her.

"No, but when we—" He cut off. There was no point in getting into this. "Never mind. Do you want me to take the picture home and wrap it, or do you want to do it?"

She dropped her hand from his arm. "I— Um— I'm not sure I can get it into my place by myself without breaking it. If you want to help me carry—"

"That's all right. I'll wrap it."

"You're sure you don't mind?"

"I don't mind," he said stiffly. "It was supposed to be my job in the first place." Was that what today had been about? She hadn't thought *just a mechanic* could handle picking out a wedding gift so she'd wrangled him into shopping together?

"Okay, well, thanks." She opened her door but didn't get out. "Luke, I really am sorry. I didn't mean—"

"It's fine. I'll see you later."

"Yeah." She stepped out of the truck. "Don't forget the opera on Saturday."

"I won't."

"Okay. Well. See you then."

He nodded without looking at her. A moment later, her door slammed, and he flinched a little.

He waited for her to pull away. Then he drove out behind her, turning left when she turned right.

He sighed as he watched her car retreat in the rearview mirror. How was it that he'd been thinking kissing and she'd been thinking *just a mechanic*? Again.

Chapter 15

Madison glared at the test paper in front of her.

It was trying to kill her.

Okay, deep breath. You know this. She read the question again: Name three signs of acute respiratory distress syndrome in dogs.

Right.

She dropped her pen to her paper: 1) increased respiratory rate, 2) blue discoloration of skin and gums, 3) Luke.

Wait. Had she just written *Luke*? She flipped her pencil over and erased furiously.

That stupid man had refused to get out of her head all week.

She'd texted him on Monday to apologize again. She still couldn't believe those words, *just a mechanic*, had come out of her mouth. The moment they had, she'd wanted to rewind and start over, but it was too late. She had never meant to imply that his job was *less than*. She thought it was great that he was a mechanic. And she knew he was good at it. It was just that she could imagine that with a brother who was a doctor, his parents might play the same comparison game as hers did.

She'd explained in her text, in a way she hadn't been able to out loud, that she hadn't meant to insult him, that she respected his career choice, that she realized how vital mechanics were. It had taken her an hour to write and rewrite the thing.

His reply had been instant—so fast that she wondered if he'd even read the whole message. And it had been short—only three words. *I forgive you.*

After a twenty-minute internal debate, she'd texted him back. *Just let me know when I can make up the last two-fifths of my debt to you.*

Again, his reply had been fast. *We'll call it even.*

She hadn't heard a word from him since then. And she'd ended up mailing him a check for her portion of the wedding gift.

But now she couldn't get him out of her head, and it was starting to affect her performance on her exams.

Okay, just finish this test, and then you can go over there. Talk to him. Tell him in person that you're sorry.

She nodded to herself and returned to her test, this time writing, "3) coughing," over the faint erasure marks from Luke's name.

She managed to focus on the rest of the test and finish it just as the professor called that time was up. She turned it in, praying she'd at least passed.

An hour later, she was approaching River Falls, staring indecisively at the upcoming intersection, her windshield wipers on against the sprinkles that dotted the windshield. Should she turn left to Luke's shop? Or right to home? Now that she was faced with the possibility of actually seeing him again, she wasn't so sure. Anyway, she'd see him at the opera in two days. Maybe she could talk to him then. Or not talk to him. Once this whole wedding thing was over, she really wouldn't have to ever see him again. Sure, they might bump into each other around town and maybe at the occasional birthday party for Mel and Brad's kids. But that didn't mean they had to be friends.

Or more.

With a sigh, she flipped on her signal light and turned right. Her wipers swept back and forth over the window. Underneath their thrum, the car made that cha-cha cha-chang sound. It was getting worse by the day. She was going to have to get it in to a mechanic soon.

If only you knew a mechanic who didn't hate you.

She gritted her teeth and kept driving. The car had made it this far. She was sure it would be fine.

She made it another block before the sound changed into an awful grinding noise and a warning light on her dashboard flashed on. She may not know much about cars, but she did know enough to pull to the side of the road and shut off the engine.

Now what? Did she keep pushing it and hope she could get home? And then drive to Nashville on Saturday?

She pressed her lips together. That wasn't really an option.

She pulled out her phone and stared at it. Luke's number was right there. Wait.

So was the number for her regular mechanic. The one she'd used for years. How had Luke's arrival made her forget that there was more than one shop in town?

She hit the number with a gasp of relief.

A receptionist picked up. "Carson Automotive. How can I help you?"

Madison explained her situation, trying to describe the sound the car had made. The woman didn't comment on her sound effects, and Madison had a sudden vision of Luke's teasing laugh when she'd made the same sounds to him.

"Okay, we can get you in next Wednesday," the woman said.

"Next Wednesday?" Madison pressed a hand to her cheek, wincing as she bumped the still bruised area under her eye. "I need the car to be done by Saturday."

"I'm sorry, but we're booked solid. Would you like me to make you an appointment for Wednesday then?"

"No. Thanks anyway." Madison hung up and did a search on her phone for another nearby mechanic. But the next nearest was in Brampton, and there was no way her car could make it back that far. Of course it couldn't have broken down an hour ago, when she'd been there.

She sat tapping the phone against her hand.

She was going to have to do it.

She held her breath as she pressed the number for Luke's shop. Carson's had had a receptionist. Maybe Luke did too.

"L&M Automotive. This is Mitch."

Madison's breath jumped out of her. "Hi. Yes. I need my car fixed right away. It's making a grinding sound, and I don't know what's wrong with it, but I need to take it to Nashville on Saturday."

"Can you get it here, or do you need a tow?"

"Um." Madison ran a hand over the steering wheel, watching a raindrop slide down the windshield. "I think I can drive it there. I hope."

"What's the name?"

"Madison Monroe."

"Oh."

Madison prickled. "Oh, what?" She heard typing in the background.

"Oh . . . kay," the guy said, but Madison was sure that wasn't what he'd meant the first time. That had been an *oh* laced with significance.

He asked her a few more questions about the make and model of the vehicle, and she gave him the information he needed.

"All right. Bring it in, and we'll take a look."

Madison desperately wanted to ask if his use of "we" meant Luke was there too. Or maybe he was using the royal we.

She could hope.

"I'll be there in a few minutes."

She turned the car on again, clenching her teeth against the grinding sound.

She finally loosened her jaw as she turned into the parking lot at L&M. But then she spotted Luke's truck, and her jaw locked tighter than before. She parked in a spot near the building and took a fortifying breath before she got out of the car.

Even if Luke was mad at her, he had to appreciate the business, right?

She surveyed the building. It wasn't huge, and the paint on the outside was starting to peel away, leaving a patina of rust. Her eyes roamed to the open garage doors. There were three bays, with cars in each already. She hoped that didn't mean they wouldn't have time to get to hers today. Her gaze roved deeper into the building. Someone was bent over a workbench near the back, and her heart stopped for a second, until she realized the guy was too short to be Luke.

Maybe he wasn't here after all.

She dashed through the light rain toward what looked like an office area, making herself open the door. Once inside, she stopped and looked around the small space. To the right of the door, there were two worn leather chairs and a small table with a smattering of magazines. On the wall to her left was a large window with a view into the shop. She squinted through it but didn't see anyone aside from the guy she'd noticed from outside.

She shuffled a little farther into the room, toward the counter that ran along the length of the back. She scanned it for a bell or some way to let them know she was here. But there didn't seem to be—

A head popped up from behind the counter, and she jumped backwards a good foot, pressing a hand to her chest.

"Madison?" Luke's mouth stood agape, as if he were as startled as she was.

"Sheesh. You could make some sound back there or something. You scared me half to death."

Yeah, start by yelling at him, Madison. That's always a good idea.

"Sorry." Luke's lips didn't lift. "What are you doing here?"

"Remember that cha-chang sound I told you about?" She waited for him to laugh, but when he didn't crack a smile, she kept going. "It turned into a terrible grinding noise. I called and talked to Mitch. He said y'all would have time to take a look at it today."

Luke glanced down at the desk, and Madison moved closer, her eyes taking in the gray, grease-stained coveralls he wore. Why on earth did they make him look so good?

"Please, Luke. You have to know how sorry I am about the other day. I never meant to hurt your feelings."

"You didn't," Luke scoffed. "I can probably get to your car in a couple hours. Do you want to come back and pick it up later?"

Madison glanced at the window. She really had no desire to walk the two miles home in the rain. "I'll just wait here. If that's okay?"

Luke shrugged. "It's not glamorous."

"It's great." Madison leaned against the desk. "Really, Luke. This place is really great." She rolled her eyes at herself. Were there any other combinations of *really* and *great* she could use?

"It's a work in progress." Luke held out his hand, palm up, and Madison stared at it. Did he want her to give him five? Or maybe he wanted to hold her hand? A tingle went through her.

"Keys." Luke waved his hand around a little.

"Oh. Right." She pulled her key chain out of her purse and dropped it into his hand.

"I'll let you know what I find." Luke tucked the keys into the pocket of his coveralls and disappeared through the door that led into the garage. Madison let her eyes follow him as he marched straight to the other guy out there. The two of them had a conversation that involved a good number of head shakes on Luke's part, but after a few minutes, Luke moved to a car in the middle bay.

He disappeared under the hood, and Madison made herself move to the waiting area to take a seat. The chair was a little more comfortable than it looked, and she rummaged through the pile of magazines on the table, settling on one with a Mustang on the cover. She paged through it, her eyes straying to Luke way too often.

She finished the magazine too quickly and picked up another. But she didn't bother to open it. Instead, she let her mind wander to the summers her family had vacationed with Luke's. When they were really little, they'd played together on the beach and in the ocean. Even through middle school, it had seemed totally normal to her to hang out with him. And then, her freshman year of high school, she'd suddenly realized that he was a *boy*. And he was kind of cute.

She'd tried to ignore it at first, which hadn't been that hard, given the fact that he was three years older and seemed to have no clue she was a girl.

But the next summer, he seemed to look at her differently. They still went swimming together, still raced through the waves and splashed each other in the ocean. Still played volleyball against each other and grilled out with their families. But there was an undercurrent to it. Mild flirting. And Madison had fallen hopelessly in love. She'd convinced herself Luke had too, though neither of them said a word about it. And when they'd returned to school in the fall, Luke had gone back to his own friends, although every once in a while, he'd smile at her in the hallways.

And then Christmas had come.

They'd been at her parents' house. They were supposed to be getting drinks for everyone. But he'd pulled out a small wrapped box and handed it to her.

"What's this? Is it booby-trapped?" She'd tried to play it off as a joke because, holy cow, no boy had ever gotten her a present before.

"Open it." Luke had looked uncharacteristically serious, and she'd unwrapped the gift to find a necklace with a small gold seashell charm.

"It's beautiful," she'd whispered. "But I didn't get you anything."

Luke had gotten this funny smile on his face and leaned closer and next thing she knew, his lips pressed softly to hers.

"There." He'd pulled back before she could even register that it was her first kiss. "Now you did."

She could still feel the heat on her face, the tingle in her lips, even though it had been eleven—no twelve—years since then. She felt at her neck now, as if she'd find the necklace there, even though it had broken years ago. She let her eyes follow Luke as he moved to the driver's seat of the car he'd been working on and turned the ignition, pumping a fist in the air as the engine turned over.

She laughed out loud at the boyish gesture. Luke pulled the car forward out of the garage, and a moment later, he drove her car into the spot.

Madison watched him work for a few minutes, but it was too nerve-wracking, not knowing what he was doing or how much it was going to cost. Or what he was thinking.

She glanced around the waiting room. There had to be something else to take her mind off him.

Ah, coffee.

She moved to the small table next to the desk that held a coffee maker and a sign that said, *Please help yourself.*

The carafe was empty, but there was a water cooler right next to the table and a can of coffee and filters next to the coffee maker. She grabbed them and busied herself making a fresh pot. Maybe she could take a cup out to the garage for Luke. And one for his partner too.

By the time the coffee was done, Luke still had his head tucked under the hood of her car. She tried to read the expression on his face, but he was too far away. Carrying two coffee cups, she pushed the door into the shop open with her hip.

It smelled like grease and metal and hard work out here, but not in an unpleasant way. Madison made her way to Mitch first. He looked up from the car he was working on, greeting her with a frown that transformed into a grin. "You must be Madison." He pointed to her eye. "Luke mentioned your shiner."

Madison tried to ignore the flutter at his acknowledgment that Luke had mentioned her.

"I— Yeah. I thought you might like some coffee."

"Wow." Mitch took the cup. "That's mighty nice of you. Luke's working on your car over there." He gestured with his head. "Just be careful for the hoses. Technically, customers aren't supposed to be out here."

"Oh." Madison looked over her shoulder to the waiting area. "I can just—"

But Mitch laughed. "I think you should take that to him. Maybe it'll put him in a better mood."

Madison swallowed and nodded, wondering if Mitch knew she was the reason for Luke's bad mood. Then again, given that *oh* he'd uttered on the phone, he probably did.

She made her way toward him, stepping gingerly around miscellaneous hoses and buckets.

Luke was bent low over her engine as she reached him, and she let herself take a moment to watch him. His hands, blackened with oil, navigated the engine with confident movements. He wasn't smiling, but he looked . . . purposeful. Like he knew what he was doing. Like he enjoyed it.

"Can you fix it?" Madison asked, moving closer.

He swiveled his head toward her, as if he'd been aware of her presence all along. Madison felt that same heat from the night of the kiss slide up her face.

"Don't drink that." He pointed to the coffee in her hand. "It's like eight hours old."

"I made a fresh pot," she said, holding it out to him. "This is for you."

He stared at her. "You know how to make coffee?" The slight note of teasing was undercut by the sharpness in his tone.

"What's that supposed to mean?" She pulled the coffee closer to her. He was going to have to make this right if he wanted it.

He shrugged. "I just figured the maid always did it for you."

104

Madison blinked back the surge of heat in her eyes. That was totally unfair. She'd been used to it from other people. Not from him. "Your family had a maid too," she shot back.

"Yeah, but I didn't make her do everything for me."

She glared at him. "Fine. Don't drink it."

"No, I'll—"

But she lifted the cup to her lips and took a long swallow, ignoring the sear of the liquid against her taste buds. "Can you fix my car or not?" Every syllable singed her tongue, but she refused to let it show.

"I can fix it," he said evenly. "But I need to order a part. It should be in by the middle of next week."

"Next week?" Madison nearly dropped her coffee. "The opera is this weekend. Do you have a loaner I can use?"

Luke frowned. "No. That's on the list of things to get."

"Fine. I guess I can ask Mel if I can ride with her and Brad to Nashville."

He stared at his boots. "I do have a vehicle, you know. And I happen to be going to the same place as you."

"Are you offering me a ride?"

He laughed shortly. "No, I'm just rubbing it in. Of course I'm offering you a ride."

She took another sip of the coffee, spluttering as it raked over her already burned tongue.

"Careful," Luke said dryly. "It looks hot."

"It is."

"So, you want a ride to Nashville or not?"

Madison pretended to think about it. But it wasn't like she really had a choice. If she asked Mel, her sister would only complain that it was out of their way to come to River Falls first.

"Fine." She took another swallow of coffee, her tongue too burned to protest anymore. "Thanks."

"I'll pick you up at two-thirty."

She nodded and started toward the door to the waiting area.

"Madison?" Luke called.

She stopped. "Yeah?"

"How are you planning to get home?" He gestured toward the garage door. The rain was coming down harder now. But she'd survive getting a little wet.

"You're not going to walk," Luke said as if she'd spoken. "I'll give you a ride. Come on." He wiped his hands on a rag. "Let me just tell Mitch."

Madison followed him, hanging back several feet so she wouldn't get in the way.

"I'll be back in a few minutes," Luke called when he was close enough. "Madison needs a ride home."

Mitch's eyes drifted over Luke's shoulder to where Madison hovered awkwardly. Madison tried not to wonder what Luke had told him about her, aside from the fact that she had a shiner.

"Did Luke show you his baby?" Mitch called to her, and Madison startled.

Luke had a baby? Why had he never—

"He means my car," Luke cut into her thoughts. "And no." He waved Mitch off. "She doesn't want to see it."

"Hey, wait a minute." Madison moved closer to the men. "How do you know I don't want to see it?"

He raised an eyebrow. "Fine. I'll show it to you. I can give you all its specs too. Since you're so interested." That wasn't only sarcasm lacing his words—it felt more like acid.

But he strode across the garage, and she took one last helpless look at Mitch. He grinned and winked at her, gesturing for her to follow Luke.

"Here she is." Luke sounded bland as he gestured to the orange beauty. "I call her Sally."

Madison moved closer to the car. "Good name." She reached out a hand to touch it but thought better of it and stuffed her hand in her pocket instead. "She's beautiful, Luke. Did I ever tell you Mustangs were my dream car?"

Luke shrugged.

Her heart dropped a little more. She knew she had. But he didn't remember. Or didn't care.

Well, why would he? That had been a long time ago.

He crossed his arms in front of his chest. "She was in pretty rough shape when I got her. So far, I've rebuilt the engine and replaced the carburetor. Put in a new flywheel. Still have some work to do on the interior. I'm going to gut it and—" He shook his head. "Never mind. Are you ready to go? I have a lot to do yet tonight."

"Of course. Sorry." Madison let herself drink in another long gaze at the car. Luke really was talented.

He pulled his keys out of his pocket and led the way to the garage door. The rain had grown into a deluge now, raindrops pelting the already puddle-riddled parking lot. "I'll pull it up."

"You don't have—"

But he was already sprinting into the downpour. Madison debated following him. But she'd never be able to keep up—and in these shoes, she'd probably end up on her backside in a puddle.

In less than a minute, Luke was pulling up to the garage door, nosing the front end of his truck into the garage so that Madison wouldn't have to step outside at all.

Grabbing a quick breath, she opened her door and climbed in.

Water had darkened Luke's gray coveralls into a deep shade that matched the gray of the sky, and shaggy strands of wet hair fell onto his forehead. Madison almost reached to brush them away but busied her hands digging in her purse instead—though the only thing she came out with was a tube of lipstick. Now what? Did she put it on? And make him think she was even shallower than he already thought?

She stuffed the lipstick back into her purse and clutched at the strap.

Rain thrummed heavily on the windshield and the wipers swiped back and forth, unable to keep it clear. But inside the cab, it was way too quiet.

"How many more cars do you need to work on yet today?" she asked to break the painful silence.

"Three or four. Unless anything else comes in."

"It's already four o'clock," Madison said in surprise. "You're going to be working all night."

He shrugged. "Comes with the territory."

"Oh." What did she say to that? "I guess it's kind of like being a vet. If there's an emergency, you just do what you have to do. It doesn't matter what time it is. Joseph is always being called in the middle of the night. Last week, he called me in to help." She hadn't done much. Mostly adjusted lights and prepared instruments. But still, she'd been proud that he'd trusted her.

Luke nodded but pressed his lips together.

Fine. If he wanted to be like that, they could ride in silence. It didn't make any difference to her.

Thankfully, they'd already reached her apartment building.

Luke pulled up as close to the front door as he could. "See you Saturday. Two-thirty."

"Thanks." She flung herself out of the vehicle and dashed for the front door, holding her purse over her head to fend off the rain. She fumbled to unlock the door, then turned to wave to Luke. But he pulled away without so much as a glance.

Chapter 16

Luke peeled off his coveralls and tossed them on a stool. "I have to fly, man. You got the Bernelli van?"

Mitch eyed him. "Please tell me you're not going to the opera like that. Madison would not be impressed."

"I don't care if Madison would be impressed." Luke glanced down at the ripped jeans and grungy t-shirt he wore. He should have just enough time to run home, shower, and change before he had to pick her up.

"Right." Mitch's laugh followed him toward the door. "And I don't care if I never rebuild another Ford."

Luke rolled his eyes and kept walking. In the lobby, he scribbled a couple of notes in the appointment book, then moved to flip the coffee machine off. He stared at it for a moment. He hadn't meant to hurt Madison's feelings with his comment about not knowing how to make coffee the other day.

Well, actually, that wasn't true. He *had* meant to hurt her feelings. But now he felt bad about it. Even if it had only been in retaliation for her *just a mechanic* comment.

He strode out the door, squinting into the bright sunlight that had pushed out the rain of the past two days. He jogged to his truck, trying not to think about the fact that he had to spend the next three hours in it with Madison.

It only took him half an hour to shower and pull on a pair of dress pants and button down shirt. He debated wearing a tie but decided against it, although he did grab a sport coat, just in case. He dug a bag out of the closet and stuffed a pair of shorts and a t-shirt in it, along with his toothbrush, deodorant, and a book. That should be all he needed.

He had fifteen minutes to spare, and he considered reading for a few minutes, but knowing Madison, she was probably ready and pacing while she waited for him.

He jumped in his truck and made the short drive to her apartment building. He pulled into a spot near the door and then just sat. Should he text her? Call her? Go to the door?

He grabbed his phone. *I'm here*, he texted, then stared at it way too long before hitting send and tossing the phone into the console.

He closed his eyes as he waited for it to buzz back at him. Offering her a ride had been a dumb idea. But what else was he going to do? Make her hitchhike to Nashville?

At least now that he knew how she felt, he wouldn't have to worry about wanting to do something stupid like kiss her anymore.

When five minutes went by without a response to his text, he shoved his phone into his pocket and got out of the truck. He marched to the door and pressed the buzzer next to her name.

It took a few seconds, but then the speaker crackled to life. "I'm almost ready." She sounded breathless. "Come on in."

He stared at the door. He really didn't need to go inside. He was fine waiting out here. But the incessant buzzing compelled him to reach for the handle.

He knocked on the door of her apartment, trying not to think of the last time he was here. When he'd put a bag of strawberries on her face and imagined there might be a future for them.

"Come in." Her voice was distant but harried sounding.

He pushed the door open and found her frantically stuffing sodas into a cooler.

"I realized this morning that we didn't get any snacks or drinks or anything for the hotel." She didn't glance up as she grabbed a bag of ice at her feet and hefted it into the cooler. She tried to close the lid, but the bag of ice stuck up too high.

Luke crossed the room. "Here." He opened the cooler, ripped the bag open, and spread it across the dozens of cans of soda. "I think you got enough," he said dryly.

"I don't know." She lifted her head, looking frazzled, the bruise around her eye still there but not nearly as dark now. "It was all I could fit in my neighbor's wagon."

Luke stared at her, trying to make sense of her statement. "Your neighbor's wagon? You mean you walked to the store? And pulled a wagon full of sodas home?"

Madison rubbed at her temples. "And snacks."

Luke snorted, but his snort turned into a chuckle, and that turned into a guffaw.

"Hey . . ." But Madison's laugh threaded itself around his. "It's not funny." They both laughed harder.

After a second, Madison sobered. "I still have to change."

Luke took in her red sweater and jeans. She looked perfect just like that, but he kept the thought to himself.

"I'll load the cooler and bags in the truck. You go get beautiful."

Madison gave him a look, and he chomped down on his tongue.

She left the room, and he secured the lid of the cooler, hefting it with a grunt. "Yep. Definitely enough soda." He wrangled the cooler out the door, quickly loading it into the back of his truck. Then he went back for the four bags of snacks she'd packed. He was going to have to ask her how much he owed for all of this. She should have called him to help. He had a truck, for goodness' sake. She wouldn't have had to pull a ridiculous wagon through the cold. Leave it to her to think he wouldn't be any help. Leave it to her—

He froze as he stepped back into her apartment. She was standing in the middle of the living room, her jeans and sweater replaced by a floor-length emerald green dress that slid over her curves. Her hair looked like gold brushing her shoulders, and her lips were a deep red that felt magnetic.

"I think I'm ready." Madison pressed a hand to her stomach.

Luke nodded dumbly. "I think you are. I mean, you look—"

Madison smirked. "Did I make myself beautiful enough?"

He shook his head. "You look . . ." he repeated.

Madison rolled her eyes. "You already said that. I only hope it ends well." Before he could figure out exactly *how* it ended, she picked up a small suitcase and breezed past him. "Come on. We're going to be late."

He wanted to point out that it was her fault, but his tongue still didn't seem to be cooperating.

He waited for her to lock her apartment, then led her to his truck. He took the suitcase from her and tucked it into the back, then turned to open the passenger door, but she was already in the truck.

Luke let out a hard breath. *She has no interest in a mechanic,* he reminded himself. Not that he needed the reminder. Because he had no interest in her, whatever his overactive imagination might be saying right now.

He climbed into his seat, ignoring the tentative smile she sent his way.

"You're sure you've got everything?" he asked gruffly.

"Oh, don't ask me that." Madison rubbed at her arms. "I have no idea anymore."

He frowned. "Are you cold? Where's your coat?"

She smacked a hand to her forehead. "Inside. Hold on. I'll go—"

But he held out a hand. "Give me the keys. I'll grab it."

"No, I can—"

"I'll be faster. You can't run in that dress."

She glanced down as if she'd forgotten what she was wearing, then dropped the keys into his hand. "It's in the closet in the hallway. Across from the bedroom."

He nodded, then turned on the truck and cranked up the heat for her before dashing for the apartment. Inside, he went straight to the closet. But there had to be fifty jackets in it. He snorted. Why anyone would need more than one was beyond him.

He pushed hangers aside, trying to figure out which one would "go" with her dress. But he had no clue. Finally, he grabbed a gray woolen one that looked like it would hang to the middle of her thighs. He spun to go, his eyes falling on the bedroom on the other side of the hallway. It was a soft blue color that reminded him of Madison's eyes, and it smelled faintly of the perfume he'd inhaled as she'd sped past him before.

He pulled in a breath before realizing how stupid he was being. He dashed toward the door, locked it behind him, and pushed out into the cold afternoon. The sun hovered above the mountains, gilding them in gold.

Luke slowed, taking a moment to appreciate the view before he jumped back into the car, thrusting the jacket at Madison.

"Oh." She held it up. "Thanks."

Her nose wrinkled. Apparently he'd chosen the wrong one.

Well, too bad.

He threw the truck into reverse and pulled out of the parking lot.

"Did you have a good morning?" she asked.

"Yep."

"Any news on my car?"

"Nope."

She fell silent, and he clicked the radio up a little louder. They drove like that for a good hour, before she spun sideways in her seat.

"How long are you going to be mad at me?"

He let his gaze flick to her for a second. "I'm not mad."

"Yes you are." She turned and dropped back against the seat. "About what I said the other day. Even though I've apologized a million times."

"It wasn't a million times," he muttered. "And I'm not mad."

"You said you forgive me," she pointed out.

"I do." He changed lanes to pass the slow-moving car in front of them.

"You're not acting like you forgive me," Madison countered.

"I—" His hands tightened on the wheel, but he let out a long breath and relaxed his grip. "You're right. I'm sorry. I do forgive you."

"Good." Madison sighed. "I really am sorry, you know. I didn't mean it how it sounded. I think it's amazing that you're a mechanic and you're clearly great at it and I respect—"

"Hey." He touched her arm to stop her. "I know. I really do forgive you. We all say things we don't mean. Like my comment about your coffee making. I'm sorry."

She laughed. "I forgive you. Honestly, I only learned a couple of years ago."

He chuckled, grateful for the lighter mood. "What inspired you?"

She fell silent, and he glanced at her. The red of her lips stood out, pursed in thought, and he suddenly had renewed visions of kissing her. He turned them off immediately and focused on the road.

"I wanted to be more than what everyone thought of me," she said finally. "I was tired of being the family joke. So I got my own place, paid my own rent, made my own coffee. Got a job." She brushed her hair back from her face, giving a derisive laugh he was pretty sure was directed at herself. "That must sound really stupid to someone who's been married and has his own business."

He shook his head. "It doesn't sound stupid at all."

"Thanks." She shivered, wrapping her arms tighter around herself.

"If you're still cold, why don't you put the jacket on?"

"I'm fine." Madison lowered her hands, but a second later, she was rubbing her arms again.

"Seriously. The heat is as high as it goes. Put the jacket on."

"I can't," Madison shot back at him. "It's too itchy."

"It's too . . ." Luke gaped at her. "Then why did you buy it?"

"I didn't. It was a gift from my mom. I wear it when I go to her house. But I always wear a thick sweater under it."

"Oh." He felt bad suddenly. He should have gone back in to get her a different jacket. "Here." He reached his right arm behind him, feeling along the back seat. "I brought this just in case I wasn't fancy enough for the opera." His hand fell on the sport coat and he tugged it forward, pressing it against her arm.

She didn't grab it from him, so he dropped it into her lap. "You might as well put it on. I need to turn the heat down or I'm going to melt before we get there. And dissolving into a puddle makes it much harder to drive."

"Oh, sorry." Madison reached for the temperature control and twisted it until the fan quieted. She slid her left arm into the sport coat, then leaned toward him to maneuver her right arm into it.

Luke caught that same vanilla scent he'd smelled in her room, and he turned his head away to check his mirror. When he turned back, she was still wrestling with the jacket.

With a laugh, he reached over and held it for her.

"Thanks." The soft word slid between them, and Luke nodded, letting go of the jacket as she got her arm into it.

She moved back into a normal position, and the air around him felt too cold without her presence.

"I like it better when we're friends." Madison's voice was warm and light.

Luke's eyes slid to her. "Is that what we are?"

"We're practically family."

"By marriage," he growled.

"Well, yeah. But we'll probably see each other at our nieces' and nephews' birthdays and stuff. So it's better if we're able to be civil with each other."

"True." Although fighting with her made it easier to fight these other feelings that were trying to push their way through. "So, how did your exams go?"

Madison flopped against her seat. "Ugh. I swear I'm going to drop out. Or fail out."

"You're not going to drop out. *Or* fail out. You were always a good student."

Madison snorted.

"Well, a better student than me," Luke amended.

"Maybe, but not as good as Mel."

"You have to stop comparing yourself to your sister. She's not you and you're not her. You have your own gifts."

Madison puffed out a disbelieving sound. "That's questionable."

His eyes flicked to her in surprise. He'd never considered Madison insecure. "Did you see that fundraiser you put together? It was a huge hit. People had fun. The animals had fun. *I* had fun."

"You did?" She turned to him, as if that was the part that mattered most.

He waved off the question. "And you're persuasive. And you care a lot about what you do. And you're . . ." The word beautiful almost slipped out, but he held it back. "Talkative," he said instead.

She laughed. "I'm not sure if that's a compliment or not."

He shrugged. "It was meant to be."

"Okay then." He could hear the smile behind the words, though he didn't look at her. "I'll take it as one."

"Good." He fell silent, and so did she.

After a few minutes, he laughed.

"What's so funny?"

"I compliment you on being talkative, and you don't say another word."

She laughed too. "Sorry. What would you like me to talk about?"

"That's your department, not mine."

"Let's see . . ." She tapped her lip, and Luke almost reached over and grabbed her hand just to make her stop drawing his attention to her mouth. "I know. Let's play truth or dare."

Luke laughed, but the sound was way more nervous than he'd like. They'd played truth or dare all the time as kids. They both always chose dares. She dared him to eat gross foods. He dared her to say something ridiculous to a stranger.

"What kind of dares can you do in a moving vehicle?" he asked.

"None." Her light laugh moved through his veins, setting his blood coursing. "It'll have to be all truth."

He swallowed. "That sounds dangerous."

"I'll go first." Madison ignored his warning. "I'll give you an easy one to start: Did you or did you not steal my t-shirt that summer at the beach?"

A laugh erupted out of him. He'd forgotten all about that. "What t-shirt?" he asked innocently.

Her hand smacked his arm, and he laughed harder.

"You know exactly what t-shirt I mean. What did you do with it?"

He shrugged. "You mean that pink one with the unicorn on it?"

"Yes."

"Never saw it."

"Luke!" She sounded completely exasperated, but she was laughing too. "It's not funny. That was my favorite shirt."

"I know." He couldn't stop laughing. "I'm sorry."

"You sound really sorry," Madison said.

"If you dig on the beach in Hilton Head, you might find it."

"You buried it in the sand?" she gasped.

"Yeah." He held up a hand to fend off any potential repercussions. But she just looked at him open-mouthed.

"I swear, I went back and looked for it for hours, but I never found it."

"You owe me a new shirt," she said decisively.

"I'll get right on that. Okay, my turn." He considered all the things he could ask her. About her. About him. About them. "What's your favorite food?"

She tsked in disbelief. "All the things you could make me confess, and that's your question? My favorite food?"

"You want me to ask something harder? Okay, what's—"

"Nope. Too late. My favorite food is grilled cheese."

"Really?" He turned to her. "All the gourmet meals you could choose, and you pick grilled cheese?"

"It was the first thing I learned how to cook myself." She sounded both proud and defiant. "My turn: What was the end of your sentence going to be before?" The words faded at the end, and he turned his head enough to see that she was looking out her window, not facing him.

"What sentence?" Playing dumb seemed like his best bet here. He followed the map's directions to make a right turn.

Madison turned toward him, speaking slowly and deliberately. "After I changed. You came in and said, 'You look—' Twice. But you never finished the sentence. So I want to know what you were going to say. I look *what*?" Her eyes challenged him, and yet she also looked uncertain.

He let his gaze drop for a second to her dress, then turned back to the road. "I didn't finish the sentence because there are no words," he said quietly. "You look . . . incredible." But that fell far too short. "Stunning. Gorgeous."

"Stop." She shoved his arm, laughing, but he caught her hand. She made one feeble effort to pull it away but then let him lower it with his to rest on the console between them.

"My turn for a question." His thumb slid in circles over the back of her hand. He had no idea what he was doing. But he did know he didn't want to stop. "Do you remember—"

"You have reached your destination," the voice from his phone blasted into the truck.

Luke pulled his hand away from Madison so he could maneuver into a parking spot. Brad and Mel were just getting out of a car two spots down.

"We're here," Madison announced needlessly, her voice higher pitched than usual, and Luke wondered if the same nerves were zinging through her as were zapping through him like electric charges.

He let out a breath as he opened his door. It was probably for the best that he hadn't been able to finish his question: Do you remember our kiss?

They may be friends again. But that didn't mean she wanted to be more. *Neither do you*, he reminded himself.

Whatever had just happened in the truck, that had been a one-time thing. Maybe the exhaust fumes had gotten to him or something. He'd have to check it out tomorrow when he got back to the shop.

For tonight, he'd just keep his distance. And his senses.

He rounded the truck to open her door.

And all of his resolve disappeared as he helped her down, his eyes falling from her lips to the way his jacket hung, way too big but somehow just perfect, from her shoulders.

"Thanks." She looked up at him, and he almost kissed her right then and there.

"Are you guys coming or what?" Mel's voice from behind him broke the spell.

"Yeah." Madison called over his shoulder. She pulled her hand out of his, but her smile held something new.

Luke took a step backwards, wondering if his did too.

Chapter 17

Madison should have asked to switch seats with someone for the opera. She'd managed to mostly avoid Luke at dinner, squishing herself between Mel and one of the other bridesmaids. The two of them had talked right over the top of Madison the entire meal—but it was still better than the alternative of sitting next to Luke. Of risking that he'd finish that question from the drive here.

She reminded herself that she was probably making more of this than was there. He was probably going to ask if she remembered the time he'd tried to teach her to surf. Or the time they'd gotten hot dogs at that food truck and she'd thrown up afterward.

She closed her eyes. She sure hoped he didn't remember that one.

"You're not falling asleep already, are you?" Luke leaned closer and whispered, his breath on her neck sending shivers—the warm kind—up and down her spine.

"No." Madison opened her eyes. "But I have no idea what's going on."

"That's because you need your eyes open to see it."

"Thanks for the tip," she said sarcastically, tearing her eyes from him to focus on the stage, even though she knew it wouldn't help. She hadn't been able to concentrate on anything for the entire first act.

And now she definitely couldn't, with Luke this close. With his rich, warm scent drifting over her, growing more intoxicating by the minute.

"So, Rodolfo and Mimi are falling in love." Luke subtly pointed to two of the characters on the stage. "But she's sick."

Madison's eyes accidentally went to his.

"He wants her to leave so she can get better," Luke continued, his eyes searching hers. "But she wants to stay with him."

"Oh." Madison couldn't figure out how to direct her eyes back to the stage.

"Now watch." Luke leaned back in his seat, but his shoulder pressed against hers. "Mind if we share the armrest?" he whispered.

She shook her head, and he slid his arm under hers, cushioning it. His fingers curled around her hand. Madison swallowed, glancing quickly to where Mel sat on the other side of her. But her sister seemed entirely wrapped up in what was happening on the stage.

Madison focused too, letting the press of Luke's hand, the smell of his cologne, the gentle in and out sound of his breaths fade into the background, as if they were a normal part of her life. As if they'd always be there.

By the fourth act, she was completely engrossed in the story. When Rodolfo and Mimi separated, she gasped. And when a dying Mimi came back to Rodolfo, she had to pull her hand out of Luke's to wipe away the tears.

His arm slid around her shoulders. He squeezed and tugged her in closer to him.

Madison let her head fall on his shoulder.

She was an emotional wreck from the show, and the armrest was digging into her ribs, but it was possibly the most comfortable she'd ever been in her life.

"Call." Brad tapped his cards on the table.

Luke eyed his brother, then his own cards. He'd already lost nearly every hand tonight. Good thing they were only playing for pocket change.

Normally, he was a decent player. But normally, he wasn't totally distracted by thoughts of a beautiful woman across the hall.

Man, he longed to have his arm around her again. To feel the weight of her head on his shoulder. To smell the warm vanilla of her hair.

"Fold." He dropped his cards to the table and pushed his chair back. He needed to take a walk or something. "I'll be back in a little bit."

"Where are you going?" one of the guys asked.

"Need some fresh air."

"He's just a sore loser," Brad called behind him.

Luke shrugged and closed the door. His brother wasn't wrong about that, but tonight he couldn't have cared less about the outcome of the game.

At least not the one going on in the hotel room.

He cared more about the game that seemed to be going on between him and Madison. She'd held his hand, settled in on his shoulder, but the moment the house lights had come up, her head had jerked away, and she'd looked around as if to make sure they hadn't been caught. Luke had tried to take her hand as they'd filed into the aisle, but she'd scooted out of his reach—intentionally or not, he couldn't tell.

And now he was standing here, in the hallway of their hotel, staring at the door of the girls' suite. Giggles came from inside, and he tried to pick out Madison's laugh, but he couldn't. He should just knock and ask her to come out here.

And then what?

He shook his head and started down the hall at a brisk pace, pulling out his phone to check the time. It was just after one a.m. Maybe not the best time for taking a stroll outdoors. But the building felt too stuffy, too confined all of the sudden. He could at least sit by the outdoor pool. Clear his head.

When he got to the elevator, he jabbed at the button for the ground floor, the slow ride down giving him way too much time to think.

When it finally stopped, he strode purposefully out the exit to the pool area. He scanned the space, relieved to find he was finally alone. But then he spotted a figure in a lounge chair tucked into the shadows behind a row of planters.

His heart jumped, but he told it to get back under control.

The person had her back to him, and though she was blonde, the chances that it was Madison—

The woman glanced over her shoulder, and he told his heart to go ahead and speed back up.

"What are you doing out here by yourself?" He didn't mean to sound gruff, but it was the middle of the night. What if some creep had followed her out here?

She lifted her face, her lips seemingly torn between a smile and a frown. "I needed some peace and quiet. It's loud up there."

"Yeah." He sat on the edge of her lounge chair. "Plus, I keep losing at poker."

She laughed, moving her legs. They bumped against his back.

"Sorry." But she didn't move them away.

His eyes went to her leggings and plain pink sweatshirt. "Put a unicorn on this shirt, and it'll be just as good as your old one." He plucked at her sleeve with a grin.

"Don't try to get out of buying me a new one," she warned. "What I don't understand is why you took it. Unless you wanted to wear it." She snickered, as if picturing him in the tiny t-shirt.

"No. If you must know, I wanted to see you in your swimsuit longer."

Madison laughed and shoved his arm. "You did not. You barely noticed that I was a girl."

He snorted. "Trust me, I noticed." He looked away, suddenly way too aware that she was no longer a girl. She was a woman. A gorgeous, intelligent, amazing woman.

"Anyway, you're the one who didn't notice me," he argued. "Not with your monster crush on Joseph Calvano."

She snorted. "Please. I had a crush on *you*. My crush on Joseph only started because you couldn't stop talking about all the hot girls you wanted to go out with."

He looked at her in surprise. "You had a crush on me?"

She bit her lip but nodded. "Stupid of me, since I was the only girl you didn't notice."

Luke shook his head, grabbing her hands. "You don't think I noticed you? I kissed you, Mads."

She looked toward the pool. "And then ignored me the very next day."

"That was because I knew you'd never go out with me."

"Based on what? The fact that I followed you everywhere you went?" Her eyes came to his.

Luke swallowed, looking away. Maybe it was time to just get this out there. "Remember later that night? We were playing Life, and I got the mechanic career, and I confided in you that I wanted to be a mechanic. Not a lawyer like my parents wanted." Luke let himself turn to her. Her eyes were on his face, and he couldn't tell if she remembered this or not. "You were the first person I told. And you asked why I'd want to waste my life like that."

Madison's eyes widened, and her mouth opened. "Oh my goodness, Luke. I don't remember— But I probably—" She blew out a breath and touched his arm. "I'm so sorry. I was a stupid kid. I thought I knew everything. Clearly not true." She shook her head. "Why didn't you say anything?"

He shrugged. "I was a stupid kid too." He slid a hand to her cheek. "But I'm not a kid anymore," he said, watching her eyes.

"No." Her whisper drew his gaze to her lips. "Neither am I."

"No," he whispered back. "You're definitely not." He slid his hand under her hair, cupping the back of her neck in his palm, drawing her closer. She inhaled sharply but closed her eyes and tilted her head.

Luke let his own eyes fall closed as his lips met hers. They were warm and full and responded instantly to the contact. Her hands slid around his shoulders, and she sighed, leaning into him.

When they pulled apart, all he could do was look at her.

"I have to say," he rasped, when he'd finally found his voice, "I think our second first kiss was even better than our first first kiss."

"I don't know." Madison's smile held mischief. "Younger you was pretty smooth."

"And older me isn't?" Luke grabbed her hands in his. "Maybe I need a second *second* kiss to redeem myself."

"Technically, we never had a *first* second kiss," Madison pointed out. "So this would be—"

"I'm going to kiss you again," he interrupted. He didn't care if it was their first second kiss or their second second kiss or their thousandth kiss. All he knew was that he wanted to keep kissing this woman for a long time to come.

"Okay," she whispered, the warmth in her eyes lighting him up from the inside out.

He moved in slowly this time, letting himself watch every play of expression over her face. When her eyes fluttered closed, he let himself trace the outline of her lashes with his fingertip, then let it trail down her cheeks to her lips before replacing it with his lips.

This was . . . *more than you asked or imagined.* The words floated into his head, and he felt his lips lift in a smile even as their kiss deepened.

The sound of a door banging open, followed by a loud voice, only vaguely registered in the back of Luke's mind—until Madison jerked away, giving him a shove that almost sent him toppling off the chair.

He blinked at her. "What's—"

But she jumped to her feet. "Over here." She sounded breathless, which made Luke grin.

It took him a moment to realize that she was calling to a bridesmaid who stood on the other side of the potted trees that cloaked them in shadow. Madison scurried toward the door.

"Oh, good. Your sister was sure you were murdered or something."

Madison's laugh was shaky. "Nope. Not murdered. Just getting some fresh air."

"Aren't you cold? It's freezing out here."

"Nope. I stayed plenty warm."

Through the trees, Luke saw her turn and look over her shoulder toward him. He laughed low in his throat. He was pretty warm too.

"Well, you should come inside," the bridesmaid said. "Mel wants to go to bed."

"Um . . . Yeah, okay." Madison looked toward him again.

He lifted a hand to wave, and she smiled, a soft smile that made his insides go all melty.

And then she followed the bridesmaid into the building.

Luke lay back on the lounge chair, staring up at the stars and grinning.

Eighteen-year-old him may have been an idiot. But thirty-year-old him was determined not to screw this up.

Chapter 18

Madison dropped a blueberry muffin onto her plate, searching the hotel's breakfast area yet again for Luke. Maybe he'd come down earlier. Or maybe he wasn't awake yet. Or maybe—

Her breath caught at the same time an invisible force lifted her lips into a smile. Maybe he was right there, in the doorway.

He grinned back at her.

And then she panicked. What if everyone realized that they'd kissed? What if they suspected they were together?

Wait. *Were* they together?

Yes, they'd kissed. But they'd kissed twelve years ago too, and look what had come of that.

A whole lot of nothing.

Luke started across the room, and Madison was frozen. He grabbed a plate and stood next to her.

"Good morning." He leaned close and kept his voice low. "How'd you sleep?"

"Um." Madison swallowed. "Good." Once she'd gotten her heart to settle down to a normal rhythm again, anyway.

"Good." He grabbed two orange juices out of the little refrigerator and passed her one.

"Thank you."

"You're welcome. I thought we'd leave after breakfast. If that works for you?"

She nodded dumbly, and he smiled again, then strode across the room to sit by one of the guys.

Madison stared after him. Was she supposed to follow? Or was she supposed to pretend nothing had happened?

Was *he* going to pretend nothing had happened? Or maybe it *had* been nothing to him. Again.

Her insides roiling, she veered to Mel's table.

Her sister eyed her. "What's wrong with you?"

"Nothing." Madison shoved a giant bite of muffin into her mouth.

"Good. We can't afford for you to get sick right now. The wedding is only two weeks away."

"Thanks for your concern." Madison rolled her eyes.

"You know what I mean." Mel brushed off her sarcasm. "You don't want to be sick for the big day. Although maybe I should line up a backup, just in case. Like an understudy." She pulled out her phone and tapped away. "I'll do that on the way home."

Madison ducked her head so her sister wouldn't see her roll her eyes again. There was prepared, and then there was obsessive.

Breakfast was over way too quickly and then they were packed up and saying their goodbyes, and Madison was climbing into Luke's truck. She folded her hands in her lap as she watched Luke move to his side of the truck. She wasn't going to assume he wanted to hold her hand, the way she'd assumed he'd want to have breakfast together.

"I think everyone's gone," Luke said as he got into the truck. "I've been waiting for this moment all morning." He reached for her hands, untangling them and letting his fingers intertwine with hers. "That's better," he sighed. "I figured we probably shouldn't steal Mel and Brad's thunder by letting everyone know about us just yet."

"Oh." That made perfect sense, and yet— "You . . . aren't going to pretend last night didn't happen?"

He blinked at her, frowning, though he didn't release his grip on her hand. "Do you want me to pretend last night didn't happen?"

She shook her head.

"Good. Because I was kind of hoping it would happen again." He tugged her closer, and she had no desire to resist. "Like right now." He dropped his lips onto hers, and she inhaled, pulling him closer.

"I was hoping it would happen again too," she murmured, resting her forehead on his.

"In that case, can I take you to a movie when we get home? And maybe out to dinner."

"That sounds nice."

"Good." He kissed her again, slow and deep, then turned on the truck and pulled into traffic.

They talked all the way back to River Falls—about her finals and the clinic, about his shop, about their families. Everything except his ex-wife. Madison tried once, but the hard set of his jaw and his monosyllabic answer led her to retreat. Instead, they rehashed memories of their summers and Christmases together.

They'd just reached River Falls when Madison's phone buzzed with a text. She lifted it absently, expecting an ad of some sort or another.

911. Pepper-broken leg. Cocoa-GDV. Need you to assist ASAP.

Madison gasped.

"Everything okay?" Luke reached for her hand again, but she was pulling on the shoes she'd kicked off earlier.

"No. I need to get to the clinic. It's an emergency."

Silently, Luke pulled his hand back, his jaw hardening. "What kind of emergency?"

"Pepper broke her leg. And Cocoa has bloat."

"And the vet can't handle it himself?" Luke sounded derisive, but Madison didn't have time to worry about that right now.

"Not both at once. Bloat is serious. Life-threatening. You can just drop me off at the clinic. I'll have Joseph give me a ride home later."

"Right." Luke's voice was subdued.

She touched his arm. "I'm sorry we won't be able to do the movie. I'll call you when I get done. Maybe we can still go to dinner. I'll get my bag from you then."

He nodded stiffly, the tension radiating from his shoulders all the way down to his forearm. "I'll probably be at the shop. I'm not sure if I'll have time."

"Oh." Madison bit her lip, trying to figure out what was going on. He wasn't mad that she had to help save two dogs, was he?

They'd have to talk about it later, because Luke was just pulling into the parking lot at the vet. She gathered her purse into her lap, ready to bolt for the building the moment they stopped.

"Thanks for the ride," she said awkwardly as Luke slowed. "And for . . ." She wanted to say *the kisses*, but the way he gripped the steering wheel made her change her mind. "I'll call you later."

"Sure." He put the truck in park, and she gave him one more look before she jumped out.

She didn't want to leave things like this. But the two injured dogs couldn't wait.

It's an emergency.

The words ticked through Luke's head over and over again. He turned the music up louder and shoved his head back under the Mustang, but it didn't help. Now the words just bounced to the rhythm of the song.

He shook his head at the irony. Two women. Same expression.

A work emergency.

You're being an idiot, a voice somewhere far in the back of his mind tried to shout. *Madison really did have an emergency.*

But that was what he'd told himself about Cindy over and over again. And Madison had always had a crush on Joseph. Hadn't she told him that a thousand times? Sure, she could claim it was because Luke had talked about other girls. But that didn't make it any less real.

When she was talking about her job on the drive home from Nashville, every other sentence had started with Joseph's name. Luke had told himself it was nothing—Joseph was her boss, after all. It was only natural that conversations about her work would involve him.

But he'd told himself that about Cindy and her boss too. That was how people got away with affairs.

Madison wouldn't do that, the voice argued more forcefully. *She wouldn't have an affair with a married man.*

Right. And neither would Cindy. Until she did.

The music cut off abruptly, and Luke pulled his head out from under the hood of his Mustang.

"You trying to lose your hearing?" Mitch stood next to the radio.

Luke shrugged. "Sorry."

"So . . ." Mitch moved closer. "How was the weekend?"

"It was fine," Luke growled.

"Yeah, I can see that." Mitch held up his hands, taking a step backwards. "What happened?"

"Nothing." Luke tossed down his wrench. "We kissed. I asked her out. She blew me off for a work emergency."

Mitch winced. "You don't think it was an emergency."

Luke shrugged. Maybe it was. Maybe it wasn't. At this point, he wasn't sure it mattered.

His phone rang, and he pulled it out of his pocket.

Madison.

He stared at it.

"Maybe it really was an emergency." Mitch raised his eyebrows.

Luke let the phone keep ringing.

"Come on, man. Don't let your stupid pride get in the way. Answer it."

Luke stared at her name.

"Hey, if you're not going to answer it, I will." Mitch took a step toward him. "I'll go out with a pretty girl like that any day."

Luke jerked his phone out of Mitch's reach.

"That's what I thought." Mitch stared him down. "You like her. Don't be an idiot and blow this."

The phone stopped ringing.

"Call her back," Mitch urged.

Luke weighed the phone in his hand. Then he stuck it in his pocket and went back to his Mustang.

Chapter 19

Madison swiped angrily at the tears on her face, then peeled her clothes off and stepped into her coziest pair of flannel pajamas.

She was *not* crying about Luke, she told herself.

She was crying about Cocoa. Joseph had tried so hard—and she'd done everything she could, though mostly she'd felt useless—but the dog hadn't made it. Watching Joseph break the news to Mr. Germain had made Madison question everything about her plans to become a vet tech.

The only thing that had gotten her through it was knowing that she could talk to Luke when she was done. Knowing that he would hold her and comfort her.

But she'd called him three times in the past two hours and texted him twice.

At first, she'd been worried when there was no response. And then she'd realized—he was ignoring her. Again.

She blew out a hard breath as the tears dropped again.

Man, she was stupid. The first time, when they'd kissed as teens, she could brush off as a schoolgirl mistake.

But this?

She wasn't a schoolgirl anymore. She *knew* better.

And she'd fallen for him anyway.

What she needed was some ice cream and then bed.

She dragged herself to the kitchen, but when she pulled the freezer open, all she found was that stupid bag of strawberries he'd placed so carefully on her bruised eye.

She slammed the freezer shut.

She might as well just go to sleep.

Numbly, she flipped off the lights and dragged herself back to the bedroom, dropping face-first onto the bed.

She closed her eyes, but tears leaked out from under her lashes and she couldn't shut off the montage of Luke's smile and Mr. Germain's glassy nod and Luke's kiss and Cocoa's still form and Luke's hand in hers.

She flipped to her side and tried again.

And then onto her back.

She was just flipping to her other side when the buzz of her intercom made her jerk upright. She listened but didn't hear anything. Someone had probably hit the button for the wrong apartment.

She lay back down but a second buzz—followed immediately by a third—had her pushing the blankets off and padding toward the door.

She grumbled as the intercom buzzed again right as she reached it. She jabbed a finger into the button. "Can I help you?"

"Madison?"

She closed her eyes. His voice wasn't supposed to still have the power to make her stomach jump like that.

She should tell him to go home. But no words came out.

"Can I come in? Please?" He sounded tentative. "I want to—"

But she'd already pressed the button to let him in. She didn't have the energy to try to convince him to go home. And, in spite of everything, she wanted to see him. Wanted to ask him why he'd ignored her after their kiss—again.

She flipped on the light, squinting against the sudden brightness. It was too much. She flipped it back off and plugged in the Christmas lights instead.

But that seemed too romantic. So she flipped the overhead lights back on too.

A soft rap on the door made her jump, even though she was expecting it.

She swiped at her face one more time—fortunately the tears had slowed a while ago, and though her cheeks were sticky, they weren't wet anymore—and pulled the door open.

"What do you want, Luke?" She crossed her arms in front of her, remembering only as Luke grinned and looked her up and down that she was wearing her flannel pajamas.

"Those are cute. Sorry if I woke you."

"You didn't." She stepped back and gestured for him to step into the room.

She considered moving to the couch before she tipped over from exhaustion, but she didn't want him to get the impression that she was inviting him to stay.

"What do you want?" she asked again.

"I wanted to— Have you been crying?" He took a step closer, his face creasing into concern.

She shook her head, but the tears started to fall again, and she had to tuck her chin to her chest.

"Ah man, Madison. I really screwed this up, didn't I?"

She sniffed, looking away from him. "I'm not crying about you." She had to make that clear. "Cocoa died."

"Oh, Mads." Before her next heartbeat, his arms were around her. "I'm so sorry."

She shook her head, trying to wiggle away and get her crying under control at the same time. But he held on tighter, pressing her head into his shoulder and smoothing her hair.

She closed her eyes, unable to fight it. She'd had to work so hard not to let Joseph see her tears—he was her boss, and he needed to know she could handle things like this—but with Luke, she didn't have to hide it. She could let him comfort her.

Wait. No, she couldn't. Because it might be comforting in the moment, but he'd already shown that he wasn't in this for the long haul.

She pushed away from him and wiped the tears off her cheeks. "Why did you come?"

"Madison, I—" He ducked his head but then met her gaze. "I'm sorry. I shouldn't have ignored your calls before."

Madison dropped into a kitchen chair. She'd known he was ignoring her, but hearing him confirm it sapped the last of her energy. "It's fine," she said dully. "It's not like we're . . ." She waved a hand around, searching for the word. "Anything."

"Maybe not." Luke moved to the table and grabbed the chair from the other side, setting it in front of her. He sat so that they were knee to knee and took her hands in his. "But I want us to be something."

She shook her head. "You have a funny way of showing it."

He blew out a loud breath. "I know. And I'm sorry. I just— My ex—"

Madison froze. He'd never spoken about his ex before.

But he looked away. "Never mind. Anyway, I—"

Madison pulled her hands out of his and stood. "You don't get to clam up again. If we're going to be . . . something." She swallowed, working not to let hope overtake her. "Then you have to be willing to talk to me. Even about the hard things."

Luke stared at the table, but his Adam's apple bobbed, and a second later, he nodded. But he didn't say anything, and Madison sighed.

"I'm tired, Luke. I'm going to go sit on the couch. If you want to talk to me, you can come join me. Otherwise, you can show yourself out." She shuffled to the couch and collapsed onto it, curling her feet under her and resting her head on the plush armrest.

Oh, that felt good.

She closed her eyes, and this time, no visions flitted behind her eyelids.

She listened, trying to tell if Luke was coming to join her. But she didn't hear a sound as the heaviness pulled her toward sleep.

Chapter 20

"Mads?" Luke whispered, standing over the top of her curled form. "Are you awake?"

There was no reply, except a soft exhale.

He smiled and brushed a strand of hair off her still splotchy cheek. It killed him to see her so upset—and to know it was at least in part his fault. He'd almost ruined everything with her.

Or maybe more than almost.

He glanced toward the door. He could leave now and try to explain everything tomorrow.

But somehow, he knew that if she woke up and he had disappeared on her again, he wouldn't get another chance.

He grabbed a blanket off the back of the couch and pulled it over her, pausing to tuck it around her shoulders.

She sighed, and he froze. But she didn't stir.

He crossed the room and flipped off the lights so that only the Christmas tree illuminated the space. Then he settled in the rocking chair next to the window. He watched Madison sleep for a bit, then let his eyes close and his mind drift. He was on the sweet edge of sleep when a shriek sent him bolting out of the chair.

"What? What's wrong?" He squinted into the dark. What room was this? It didn't look like his house.

A form took shape in front of him, and he remembered. "Madison?"

"Luke." Madison had both hands pressed to her heart. "Oh my goodness. You scared me half out of my wits. What are you doing here?"

He stepped toward her. "You said if I wanted to talk, I should come in the living room. But then you fell asleep. So . . ." He gestured at himself.

"You stayed?" Madison tucked a wild strand of hair behind her ear.

"I stayed. I'm not going anywhere, Madison. I want this to work. And if that means you want me to talk, I'll talk. I'll tell you anything. I'll tell you everything."

She smiled softly. "I'm glad." She glanced over her shoulder. "But do you mind if I use the restroom first?"

His chuckle filled the space. "Go ahead."

She scurried down the hallway, and he moved into the kitchen, rummaging for bread and cheese.

"What are you doing?" Madison's voice made him smile.

"I thought you might be hungry."

"For grilled cheese? At eleven p.m.?"

"You said it was your favorite food. I didn't know that only applied to specific times." He grinned at her over his shoulder, and she smiled back.

"It smells good."

He finished the sandwiches and grabbed a couple of plates. He passed one to her, then followed her back into the living room. They both settled on the couch, though Luke made sure to give her a little distance.

Madison took a bite of her sandwich. "Almost as good as mine."

"I'll take that as a compliment." He turned to her, unsure where to go from here. "I'm not sure what you want me to say," he confessed.

"Well." Madison picked up a piece of crust that had fallen off her sandwich. "You were going to say something about your ex before. What happened between you two?"

Luke let out a breath. She was going to go straight to the heart of things. Good to know.

"Well, let's just say she made it clear she could have done better. And then she did." He hated that he could still hear the hurt in his voice.

Madison slid a little closer. Maybe talking had its benefits after all.

"I figured it out at Christmas," he continued. "We opened presents. I gave her a ring that she pretty much mocked because the gem was small. Then she got a call and said she had a work emergency." He stopped and swallowed. "It wasn't unusual. But this was Christmas. And suddenly, it just clicked. I asked her, and she admitted there was no emergency. She was seeing her boss."

"Oh no, Luke, I'm so sorry." Madison moved closer again, her hand falling on his arm. But then she pulled it back with a gasp. "Wait. Is that why you . . . You thought I was—"

Luke heaved out a sigh. "No. I mean, not really. I know you wouldn't— But it just made everything so real, and I realized that if I let myself fall in love with you, I'd be risking all of that again. And it wasn't very fun the first time, so . . . I was trying to protect myself, and in the process I hurt you, and I'm so, so sorry." He reached for her hands. "Do you think you can give me another chance?"

Madison was staring at him, wide eyed. "Fall in . . ."

He nodded, suddenly realizing that was what he wanted with Madison. To fall in love. And he was well on his way already. "It could happen. Just to warn you."

She nodded and licked her lips, and he leaned down to catch them with his own.

When he finally pulled back, he wrapped her in his arms, and they snuggled on the couch, talking until the room shifted from black to gray to gold.

As the clock turned to seven, Luke stretched and reluctantly slid her out of his arms. "I can't believe we stayed up all night talking." They'd talked about life and dreams and faith and hopes. Things he'd never talked about with anyone else. "I have to get to the shop. But can I see you tonight?"

Madison nodded but didn't get up. "I think I'm just going to stay here all day."

"I thought you had to work?"

She shook her head, and the tears that he thought he'd finally chased away filled her eyes again. "I can't do it. I'm going to call the school and cancel the classes I signed up for next semester."

Luke dropped to the couch next to her, wrapping both of his hands around hers. "Is that really what you want?"

She shrugged. "I just don't think I'm cut out for this. Maybe I'm not cut out for anything."

He laughed. "That's not true. You're cut out for me." He leaned forward and dropped a kiss on her nose, but she shook her head.

"I mean it, Luke. Maybe my family is right. Maybe I'm just the kind of person who—"

"You want to know what kind of person you are?" Luke tugged her hands until she looked at him. "You're smart and you're determined and you're strong. It's not your fault Cocoa didn't make it. I'm sure Joseph told you that." It didn't even make him wince to say her boss's name.

"Yeah," she confessed.

"And you love those animals. And you're good with them. And I know you love what you do. Sometimes it's going to be hard, but that doesn't mean you can't do it, right?"

Madison let her eyes come to his. "You're pretty good at this pep talk stuff, do you know that?"

He laughed. "Only because every word is true. Now, come on. Go get dressed and we'll stop at Daisy's for breakfast. Unless you want another grilled cheese?"

"Daisy's is good."

He laughed. "You don't like my grilled cheese?"

She grinned and scooted down the hallway. "It turns out it does apply only to specific times. And breakfast isn't one of them."

Chapter 21

Come outside. I have a surprise for you.

Madison smiled and closed her veterinary nutrition book. Studying could wait. She slid on a pair of slippers and ran out the front door.

Luke stood in the parking lot, and for a moment she was so happy to see him, she didn't even notice what he stood next to, until he held his arms out to the side.

"My car!" She jogged toward it, holding out her arms as if to hug the vehicle, but at the last second, she veered and hugged him instead.

"That's more like it." He laughed into her hair, squeezing her so hard her feet lifted off the ground. She raised her face to his for a kiss.

"Does this mean you're not going to be my chauffeur anymore?" It had taken longer than Luke had anticipated to get the part in, but that had turned out for the best. It'd given her an excuse to see him multiple times a day for the past week and a half.

"I thought maybe today *you* could be *my* chauffeur." He dropped another kiss onto her lips. "Pay back that last two-fifths you owe me from the Santa Paws fundraiser."

"I thought we called that even?" she teased.

"I changed my mind. But you're going to need warmer shoes than that. And a coat. And a hat. Didn't anyone tell you it's almost Christmas?"

"I'm surprised you're willing to admit it." She laughed and led him inside. "So where am I chauffeuring you to?"

"That's a surprise. What are these?" He eyed the chocolate covered peanut butter balls spread on her table to cool.

"Peanut butter balls. But they're only for people who like Christmas," she warned.

"Hmm. That's too bad." He snatched one off the table and stuffed it in his mouth.

"Hey!" She grabbed her jacket out of the closet. "You realize that now you have to say you like Christmas."

He shrugged. "I like the peanut butter balls." He popped another in his mouth, then came to join her in the hallway, pulling her boots out of the closet. "And—" He stood and kissed the top of her head. "I like you."

"I guess that'll do for now." She kissed him, then pulled her boots on. "But by the time this Christmas is done, you're going to be in love." Wait. Did that sound like she meant— "With Christmas, I mean," she stuttered. "You're going to be in love with Christmas." She couldn't expect him to be in love with her by Christmas. Even if she thought she might be in love with him already.

"I knew what you meant, don't worry." He kissed her again, tucked a piece of hair into her hat, and led her to her car.

"Now are you going to tell me where we're going?" she asked as she started the vehicle. "Hey, it doesn't cha-chang anymore."

"Nope."

"Nope, it doesn't cha-chang, or nope you're not going to tell me where we're going?"

"Both." Luke grinned. "But I *will* give you directions. One step at a time. You'll just have to trust me for the destination."

Madison nodded. She did trust him.

She took a left out of the driveway as he instructed, then a right, then another left to head out of town and into the mountains.

She had no idea where they could possibly be going. But it really didn't matter. Spending the day together was enough for her.

Forty minutes later, Luke told her to turn right onto what looked like an old logging road. She slowed but didn't make the turn. "Are you sure my car can handle it?"

"She can handle it," Luke said confidently.

Madison took the turn, driving slowly down the rutted lane. "What could possibly—"

Her breath caught on a laugh as she spotted the sign. "A Christmas tree farm?"

"Well, you keep telling me I need a tree, so I figured I'd make you help me pick one out and cut it down."

"I would love to." She pulled up alongside a small shed, and they got out of the car.

Luke opened her trunk and pulled out a plastic sled and a handsaw.

She laughed. "You're pretty sneaky."

"Yep." He took her hand and led her toward the rows of pine trees.

She inhaled deeply. "It smells so good here. Like Christmas and . . . and—"

"Joy," Luke filled in.

Madison looked at him in surprise, and he shrugged. "If joy had a smell."

They wandered through the trees, examining trunks and branches and needles. It took an hour, but finally they agreed on the perfect one.

Luke held his saw to the tree trunk but then turned to her. "Do you want to do it?"

She took stock of the saw. "I don't really know how."

"Well, come here. I'll teach you."

She moved closer, and he wrapped his arms around her, moving her arm back and forth so that the saw bit into the trunk. After a few strokes, he let go, leaving her to do it herself.

Her arm burned by the time she was halfway through the tree, but she kept going, and when the trunk finally gave way with a satisfying crack, they both cheered.

They loaded the tree onto the sled and pulled it to the shed to pay for it. As they struggled to lash it to the top of her car, Madison stopped. "Wouldn't it have been easier to use your truck for this?"

"Well, yeah, but then how would you pay back the last two-fifths?"

"So we're even now?"

"Nope." Luke grinned and threw her another length of rope. "This was one-fifth. The other one-fifth is helping me decorate it."

Luke took the snowflake-shaped ornament Madison held out to him and placed it on a branch.

"That was the last one." Madison scrutinized the tree. "We're definitely going to have to get you more for next year."

Next year? Luke liked the sound of that.

"But it still looks festive." Madison adjusted a string of lights.

"It's perfect." Luke moved to wrap his arms around her from behind. "This is perfect." He nuzzled his face into her hair.

"So you admit you like Christmas?" She spun in his arms, lifting her eyes to him. He traced a finger lightly over the spot where her bruise had completely healed.

"I admit it's growing on me."

"And does today go in the good Christmas memories column?"

"Definitely." He let his lips linger on hers for a moment.

"Good." She wiggled out of his arms. "Now all we need is a Christmas movie."

He groaned. "Hey, go easy on me. I already cut down and decorated a tree today."

"Actually, *I* cut it down," Madison shot back. "Come on. I'll let you help me pick."

"On my own TV? Gee, thanks." But he followed her to the couch. He was pretty sure he'd follow her anywhere.

He wrapped an arm around her, and she snuggled close as she flipped through the Christmas selections on TV. She paused on what looked like a sappy romance.

"Uh, no." He had to draw the line somewhere.

"You're no fun," she pouted.

He caught her lips between his. "What do I need with a movie romance when I have the real thing right here?"

She laughed. "Smooth. And effective. All right. How about—" Her phone rang, and he caught Joseph's name on the screen before she sat upright and swiped to answer.

Luke sat up too. He couldn't hear Joseph's end of the conversation, but Madison took his hand.

"Actually, I was—" She cut off and listened again. "No. I understand. I'll be right there." Slowly, she lowered the phone from her ear and turned to Luke, her expression pained. "I'm so sorry. I have to go. Mr. Gray's dog got into rat poison and needs a shot of Vitamin K and observation. Joseph's out of town and can't make it back for a few hours, so . . ."

"I see." Luke ran a hand through his hair.

"I understand if you can't— If this is too hard for you to adjust to. Really, there aren't usually this many emergencies, but there *are* emergencies sometimes, and—"

"Madison." He caught her hands. "It's okay. I understand. Go."

She studied his face. "You're sure you're okay with it?"

"Yes. I'm sure."

"Because Joseph won't be there?" She bit her lip, looking away.

"Because I trust you." He kissed her. "Now go. You have a dog to save."

"I'll see you tomorrow? At the rehearsal?"

"Okay, but I'm not looking forward to it."

She gave him a puzzled look.

"I won't be able to hold your hand or kiss you there," he explained. They'd already agreed it would be best to wait until after the wedding to reveal their relationship so Mel and Brad could have their big day to themselves. But now he was regretting that decision.

"Well, I guess we'll just have to make up for it with extra kisses after the wedding." Madison pressed her lips to his, then sprang up from the couch and pulled on her jacket and boots.

The moment she left, Luke was looking forward to seeing her again.

Chapter 22

"And then you turn and walk back down the aisle," Pastor Calvano said to Mel and Brad. "As husband and wife." They both nodded solemnly, and Madison wondered how they could be so calm about it. Her own heart was going crazy as she and Luke approached each other to practice walking out behind Mel and Brad, even though it was only as best man and maid of honor. She tried not to let her thoughts go to the possibility of one day walking down the aisle with him as bride and groom.

Luke held out his arm with a quirk of his eyebrow, and Madison looped her hand through it, relishing the solid feel of his muscles under her fingertips.

Luke leaned closer, murmuring into her ear, "Is it bad that I really want to kiss you right now? Maybe no one would notice."

She couldn't help the giggle but quickly sucked it back in as Mel turned to shoot her a look. "I think she'd notice," Madison whispered back. But she was almost willing to take the risk.

Their relationship may still be new, but it was already . . . more than she could have imagined. They spent nearly every free moment together. And some not-free moments too, as she watched him work on cars at his shop and he helped her study. And they talked. Oh, did they talk. Luke told her more about his marriage. Madison told him more about the various subjects she'd half-heartedly started to study before discovering her love of helping animals. And they talked about the deeper things too—about God and about faith and about what that meant for the way they lived. Madison had never been with someone who challenged her and encouraged her and strengthened her the way he did.

She reluctantly let her hand fall from his arm as they exited the church. He subtly tangled his fingers with hers for a second, then walked off to join the other groomsmen. Madison made her way to her family. They were supposed to drive together to The Depot for dinner. Her mother and Mel spent the drive analyzing how things had gone at the rehearsal, and Madison tuned them out, letting her mind trip to a place she rarely let it go: her own future with Luke. They hadn't been dating long enough to have the discussion, but sometimes she wondered if he'd ever be willing to marry again, given how terrible his first experience was.

Mel nudged her. "Did you hear what I said? You and Luke need to walk down the aisle a little faster."

"What?" She jerked her head to her sister. There was no way she knew—

"Yeah. You're holding up the line of bridesmaids and groomsmen on the way out."

"Oh. Sorry." Madison relaxed a little. "We'll go faster."

"Good." Mel went back to her conversation with Mom.

They pulled into The Depot right behind the truck full of groomsmen, and Madison's heart leaped as Luke was the first to jump out. She watched him laugh with his brother, and then they both started toward the vehicle Madison shared with her family.

He moved to her door, while Brad went to Mel's.

She panicked. What if her family got suspicious?

But no one seemed to notice, and she and Luke walked into the building next to each other. She hoped they'd be seated together—perhaps they could hold hands under the table—but they ended up across from each other, with her parents next to her and his next to him.

"So, Luke, I hear you opened a little shop," Madison's Dad said.

Madison winced. "It's not a little shop, Dad. It's great. You should see the Mustang he's restoring."

Luke sent her a warm look she felt all the way to her toes.

"Yeah?" Dad sounded interested. "What year?"

"1969," Luke answered.

"What about you, Madison?" Luke's mom asked. "Your mother tells me you're doing some part-time secretarial work for Dr. Calvano?"

Madison tensed. "For now. I'm actually—"

"Here we go again." Mom dabbed her mouth with her napkin.

"Here we go *what* again?" Madison shot back, trying but failing to keep her voice even, reminding herself this wasn't the time or the place.

Her mom took a sip of water. "I was just thinking the other day that it was about time you'd be getting bored and flitting to your next—"

"Actually," Luke jumped in. "Madison won't be a secretary for long because she's studying to be a vet tech."

Madison glared at him as her parents both turned to her.

"Really?" Her mother sounded skeptical. "And what does a vet tech do?"

"Oh. Um—" Madison seemed to have completely forgotten. "Helps the vet. Mostly with little—"

"Actually," Luke jumped in again, frowning at her. "She's already assisted Dr. Calvano with a couple of surgeries. She helped save Mr. Gray's dog just last night." The pride in his voice melted away Madison's anger that he'd spilled her secret.

"Really?" This time it was Dad who spoke. "Gray loves that ugly dog. I don't know what he would do if something happened to it." He shot her a look that Madison thought may be approval.

"And how do you know so much about this, Luke?" his mom asked with a small smile, her eyes moving from her son to Madison.

"Oh. Uh."

Madison wondered if his face felt as hot as hers.

"Madison had her car in the shop, and we got to talking. That's all." But the way he looked at his plate and mumbled only made his mom perk up more.

"I see," was all she said, but the gleam in her eye said she saw more than he'd spoken.

Mel nudged Madison. "Come to the ladies' room with me?"

Madison's heart sank. She hadn't meant to ruin Mel's night. "Of course." She pushed her chair back and shot Luke a panicked look before following her sister to the restroom.

Inside, Mel turned to her with her arms crossed. "Do you two really think you're fooling anyone?"

"I— We— Who two?"

Mel laughed. "Madison. Everyone out there, with possibly the exception of Mom and Dad, knows that you and Luke are together."

"We're not—" But Madison broke off at her sister's fierce glare. "I'm sorry, Mel. We were trying to hide it until after the wedding."

"Why?" Mel sounded genuinely confused.

"Well, I mean, it's your special day. And we didn't want to take any of the attention from you. Not that I think we would, but you know how it can be when people learn about a new couple." She couldn't help the grin that lifted her lips at the word *couple*.

Mel blinked at her. "It's not a competition, Madison. You being happy doesn't make my special day any less special. If anything, it makes it more special."

"Really?"

"Really." Mel rolled her eyes. "What kind of sister do you think I am? I mean, besides a bridezilla."

Madison laughed. "You're far from a bridezilla." She stepped forward to hug her sister.

"Come on, let's get back out there so poor Luke and Brad don't have to deal with the parents by themselves." Mel grabbed her hand and pulled her toward the door. "Oh, and it's really great that you're studying to be a vet tech. You're going to be awesome at it."

Madison opened her mouth to say thank you, but no words would come out past the lump in her throat. All these years, she'd assumed Mel thought she was better than Madison. But maybe that had been Madison's own insecurities. She squeezed her sister's hand and followed her toward the table.

Halfway there, they ran into Luke.

"Going somewhere?" Mel asked with a laugh.

"Oh. Uh. I was just—" Luke sent Madison a look that pleaded for help.

"I'll leave you two alone." Mel patted his arm and disappeared.

"All the parents have been grilling me," Luke hissed. "I think I managed to throw them off, but I'm not sure how much longer I can—"

"They know." Madison slid her hand into his.

"No. I was really—"

"Mel knows," Madison amended. "And Brad. The whole wedding party. She's pretty sure your parents do. And they're probably telling my parents right now. Apparently, we're not as covert as we think we are."

Luke laughed. "There goes that career in the CIA I was hoping for. But on the bright side, does that mean I can kiss you now?"

"Not if I kiss you first." Madison popped onto her toes and wrapped her arms around his neck, sighing as their lips met. Across the restaurant, their table burst into applause. Madison just laughed and kept kissing him.

Chapter 23

It was Christmas.

Luke waited for the heaviness that had overcome him the last few Christmases to wash over him. But all he felt was joy.

He popped out of bed and got ready quickly, then grabbed the present that had been sitting tucked under the tree for a week, driving Madison crazy, and hopped into his truck.

He pulled into the parking lot of Beautiful Savior, waving to the people who had become familiar faces. After so long wandering, it felt good to have a church home again.

He scanned the parking lot, smiling when he saw Madison's car pull in. He jogged to the spot she angled her car into and opened the door the minute she'd turned off the engine.

"Merry Christmas." He waited impatiently for her to get out of the car.

"Well, look who's in a Christmassy mood." Madison laughed as she stood and Luke gathered her into his arms, squeezing tight and burying his face in her hair. Maybe they should just stay right here all day.

But she kissed his cheek, then grabbed his hand. "Come on, let's get inside."

She wrapped her hand around his arm and let him steer them toward the church.

"Mel texted this morning," she said. "To say Merry Christmas. Apparently it's a balmy eighty degrees in Cozumel right now." She shivered against the decidedly cooler temperatures out here, and he wrapped an arm around her. "And she thanked us again for the picture we got them. I think they really do like it."

"Of course they do. We make a good team. Brad said they're going scuba diving today." That sounded fun enough, but Luke was more than content to be right where he was—with Madison.

Inside, they made their way to the pew where Madison's parents had saved them a space. They all exchanged greetings, and it wasn't until they finished that Luke realized they were seated behind the Calvano crew. It looked like the whole family had made it home for Christmas.

"Merry Christmas." Ava turned around and smiled at both of them.

Joseph turned too, and offered a hand to Luke. "Merry Christmas."

Luke nodded and shook his hand. "Merry Christmas."

"Merry Christmas, you two," Madison said, sliding her hand into Luke's. It was freezing, and he rubbed it to warm it up as the service started.

When Pastor Calvano stood to deliver his sermon, Luke shifted his arm to wrap it around Madison's shoulder, and she snuggled in closer to him. He kissed the top of her head, soaking in Pastor Calvano's message that "We love because he first loved us." It was true, Luke knew, but he'd never really gotten that before. He'd always thought maybe he wasn't good enough for God or maybe there was some cosmic scorecard and he was losing. But now he saw it: he hadn't done anything to earn God's love. He *couldn't* do anything to earn God's love. And yet God loved him anyway. And he'd sent this beautiful woman at his side to help him see that. More than that, he'd sent him Jesus, to take away his sins.

By the time the service was done, Luke's heart was ready to burst with joy. And with love. God's love for him, and—

He turned to Madison. "Come on. I want to give you your present."

Madison laughed. "I told you that you could give it to me last night, but you refused."

"That would be cheating. It wasn't Christmas yet." He was about to pull her to her feet, but Joseph turned around.

"Hey, I hate to ask this, but could you swing by the clinic and check on Sable and the puppies? I'll take the nighttime shifts."

"Of course." Madison turned to Luke. "You'll come with me, right?" He couldn't quite interpret her smile, but he wasn't about to say no to going anywhere with her.

"Fine," he pretended to grumble. "But I get to give you your present as soon as we're done there."

"Deal." She squeezed his hand, and Joseph thanked them as they headed for the parking lot.

"Let's take my truck. Your present is in there. Do you need to get anything out of your car?"

"Nope." She still wore that strange smile.

"What's going on?"

"Nothing."

"Hmm." He kissed her, then opened her door and grabbed the gift off the passenger seat so she could sit down.

"Ooh. What's in there?" she asked, reaching for the box.

But he shook his head and tossed it into the back seat. "You'll have to wait and see." He got into the driver's seat and made the short drive to the clinic.

"You're coming in, right?" Madison asked. "It's too cold to wait out here."

"I'm coming in," he agreed. "But not because it's cold. Because I want to be with you."

"Good answer." She kissed him and they went to the clinic door. The moment she unlocked and opened it, the sound of mewling puppies called for them.

Madison grinned at him. "Remember that call I had the other night? It was for an emergency C-section. You have to see the puppies. They're so cute." She led him to a back room lined with kennels. In one corner, a low wall cordoned off a separate area. Eight tiny puppies lay in a pile in the middle of the space, their eyes not even open yet. A larger dog that Luke assumed must be the mom was curled on a dog bed.

"Labs?" he asked.

Madison nodded, stepping over the wall and gently lifting a pup, moving it to the mother. As the pup began suckling, Madison brought the rest over.

"Whose are they?"

"Well, Sable was Mr. Courtland's, but he passed away a couple weeks ago, and his wife knew she wouldn't be able to handle a litter, so Joseph said he'd find homes for them. I know one is already spoken for though." She picked up the last pup, a little golden pile of fur.

She held it out to him. "Merry Christmas."

"I— What?" He took the puppy and pulled it against his chest. It nuzzled its face into his neck. "You're serious?"

She nodded. "She'll have to stay with her mom for several weeks yet, but you can visit her anytime. And you can name her whatever you want. But I've been calling her Joy."

"Joy." He held the puppy out to examine her. She wriggled, her crinkly nose twitching, and Luke could have sworn she nodded. "Joy is a perfect name. Thank you." He leaned in to kiss Madison, the pup squirming between them.

He held the critter a little longer, then brought her to her mother to feed. When Madison was done taking care of the pups, he gave Joy one last scratch behind the ears. "Thank you," he said again. "This was the perfect gift."

She smiled at him. "I just figured this would guarantee you had a Christmas of Joy."

"Being with you already guaranteed that. Come on, my turn to give you your present. Although I'm not sure it lives up to a puppy." He led her to his truck and pulled the gift out of the back seat.

She dug eagerly into the paper and opened the box inside.

A laugh burst out of her. "Where did you find this?" She lifted the pink unicorn t-shirt out of the box and held it in front of her.

"Believe me, it wasn't easy." He'd scoured the internet looking for one that exactly matched the one he'd hidden from her when they were kids.

"Thank you. I love it. I'm going to put it on as soon as we get to my parents'."

"There's something else." Luke cleared his throat.

Madison ran her hands over the sparkles in the unicorn's hair. "I'm pretty sure nothing could top this shirt."

Luke reached for her hands, and she looked up at him. He swallowed.

"I love you, Madison."

Her eyes widened, and she laughed softly. "I was wrong. That definitely tops the shirt. I mean, the shirt is amazing, but—" She shook her head. "The point is, I love you too."

She leaned closer, and he brought his lips to hers, letting the kiss linger.

When they pulled apart, she grinned at him. "Is this because I gave you a puppy?"

He laughed. "No. But it doesn't hurt."

Chapter 24

"I'm so proud of you." Luke swept Madison into his arms and spun her around, sending her graduation cap flying.

"Luke!" She shrieked and clutched at his shoulders.

He set her down and promptly caught her lips in a kiss.

"Hey, there are other people here who would like to congratulate her too, if you don't mind." Joseph gave Luke's shoulder a good-natured shove.

"Well, you'll just have to wait a minute," Luke murmured, bending to kiss her again. But this time, he pulled away after a second, making room for Joseph and Ava—with whom he and Madison had become good friends over the past few months. Madison's parents and Mel and Brad and even Luke's parents followed, and although Luke was impatient for another turn to congratulate her, he couldn't be upset that so many people had come to celebrate her. She deserved it.

"Graduation lunch at our house," Melanie trilled. "Everyone is invited."

"Thanks, Mel." Madison beamed, and Luke couldn't help smiling at the way the relationship between the two sisters—and even between himself and his brother—had warmed up as they'd made an effort to spend more time together.

"I just have to go thank a couple of my professors," Madison said to the group, "but we'll meet you there."

Luke loved that whenever she spoke, it was about "we," as in the two of them.

The others left for Mel and Brad's new house, and Luke hung out under the shade of a large magnolia as he waited for Madison to say goodbye to her teachers and classmates. He reached into his pocket to make sure the gift he'd gotten her was still there, a sudden rev of 600-horsepower nerves hitting him as he spotted her crossing the grass toward him.

"Okay, I'm ready to go." Madison's smile radiated joy. "I still can't believe I did it."

"I never doubted it." Luke pulled her into the shade of the tree. "Come here. I want to give you your graduation present before we go to lunch."

"My present?" Her eyes lit up. "Did you get me another t-shirt? Because I think I'm already wearing out the one you got me for Christmas."

"Sorry, not a t-shirt."

"A puppy then, to play with Joy and tire her out?"

Luke laughed. The little pup she'd given him would need six more dogs to tire her out.

"Not a puppy." Luke pulled the little box, wrapped in gold foil, out of his pocket, holding it out to her.

"I— Oh." Her eyes came to his, but he bounced the box on his hand. "Take it."

She reached for it, but her eyes never left his.

"I think you're going to have to look at it to open it."

"Right." She ducked her head, pulling slowly at the paper to reveal the velvety jewelry case underneath.

She stared at it, not saying anything, and the anticipation almost killed Luke, but he made himself wait for her to open the box.

She did, blinking at the contents. "It's a key." She raised her eyes to his, a question in them.

"A Mustang key," he clarified.

Her eyes widened. "Luke, you can't give me Sally."

"Actually—" He stepped forward. "I was hoping we could share her. Look under the key."

"What?" Her brow wrinkled. "There's nothing . . ." But she lifted the little velvet separator the key had rested on, her gasp setting Luke's heart on fire.

He dropped to one knee, gently taking the box from her and lifting out the ring that lay in the bottom.

"Madison." He swallowed, overcome suddenly by the way God had worked all things in his time. "I don't know if you know this, but from the time we were kids, I have had the biggest crush on you."

She laughed, wiping at her eyes with a shaky hand.

"But I never could have imagined it turning into something more. But God knew. And I am so glad that when the time was right, he brought you back into my life. And I want you to be in my life for the rest of my days. So Madison Monroe, will you marry me?"

"Yes!" Her face was covered in tears now, even though she wore the biggest, most beautiful smile he'd ever seen.

He slid the ring onto her finger, then stood and engulfed her in a hug, spinning her through the air for the second time that day.

When he put her down, they stood, just looking at each other, until Luke laughed with sheer joy. "We're getting married." He grabbed her hands and pulled her to him. "Who would have imagined?"

She laughed too, lifting her face to his. "God did."

"I sure am glad about that," he murmured, before he let himself experience the joy of another kiss.

Epilogue

Madison had the vague feeling she was supposed to be nervous.

It was her wedding day, after all.

But of all the things she was feeling right now—joy, excitement, anticipation—she couldn't find nervousness among them. She couldn't wait to walk down the aisle with Luke. And then to celebrate Christmas with him in a few days. And then to enjoy every day of the rest of their life together.

"They did the flowers all wrong." Mom rushed into the room, waving her arms around. "And one of the groomsmen forgot his shoes. And Luke is no help. He says the groomsman can just wear his tennis shoes." Mom looked scandalized, and Madison laughed.

"Relax, Mom. Tennis shoes will be fine."

"They're red." Mom jabbed a hand against her hip.

"They'll match the flowers then." Madison lifted the hem of her dress and moved to Mom. "Really. I appreciate your concern. But everyone could be standing up there in pajamas and slippers, and I wouldn't care. I just want to marry Luke. The rest doesn't matter."

Mom opened her mouth, and Madison braced herself for whatever argument was next. But instead, she snapped it shut, her eyes traveling up and down the length of Madison's dress. Madison ran a hand over the simple embroidery on the bodice. It was her favorite part.

"You look beautiful." Mom stepped forward, wrapping Madison in her arms.

"Oh." Even though her relationship with her mother had improved over the past few months as they'd planned the wedding together, the hug was still unexpected, and it took Madison a moment to lift her arms to her mother's back.

But when she did, tears pricked her eyes. She and her mother may not be super-close yet, but she was grateful for the strides they'd made.

"I'm so proud of the woman you've grown into." Mom pulled back and there were tears in her eyes too. "I wish nothing but happiness for you and Luke. Well, that and lots of grandbabies you can bring over to my house."

"What, this one isn't enough for you?" Mel waddled into the room, resting a hand on her belly, which protruded under the dark green bridesmaid dress. She and Brad hadn't planned to have a baby so quickly, and it still astonished Madison how eagerly Mel had accepted and even embraced this change to her plans.

"It's a good start," their mother said. "But I'm going to need a lot more grandchildren than that. I figure we need at least two doctors, one lawyer, maybe a couple of investors . . ."

"Mom," Madison and Mel both exclaimed.

Mom laughed. "I'm kidding. I'm kidding."

The door opened before Madison could respond, and Ava sailed into the room, her dress the same color as Mel's but a slightly different style. "We're ready." She smiled at Madison. "You look stunning."

"Thank you." The nerves that had been absent all morning suddenly hit Madison right in the middle.

This was big.

Bigger than graduating from school.

Bigger than planning the Second Annual Santa Paws Pictures, which had gone off without a hitch last week, with Luke reprising his role as Santa—and Joy making friends with every single dog in town.

This was the biggest thing she'd ever done.

A lifetime commitment.

To Luke.

She let out a breath, and all the nerves disappeared.

He was the man she wanted to be with, for better or worse and everything in between.

"It's going to be wonderful." Mom kissed her cheek and disappeared, and Mel hooked her arm through Madison's. "Come on. Let's go get you married."

She led Madison to their father, whose eyes were shining.

"Dad?" She'd never seen his eyes so much as water before, not even at Mel's wedding.

"I'm proud of you, Madster." His use of the funny nickname he'd called her as a girl made the tears fall from her eyes.

"And I'm happy for you." Dad hugged her, then cleared his throat and held out an elbow, all business again as the wedding procession moved from the lobby into the sanctuary.

The moment Madison was in the church, her gaze landed on Luke, although the tears blurring her vision made him look wobbly.

It wasn't until her dad had kissed her cheek and passed her hand to him that she realized there were tears on Luke's face too.

"You're crying," she whispered.

He laughed quietly. "You are too." He tucked her hand into his arm, and they made their way together to where Pastor Calvano waited.

As the pastor delivered his message on their chosen verse, Nehemiah 8:10, "The joy of the Lord is your strength," Madison couldn't stop smiling through her tears. She and Luke had found joy, not only in each other, but in the Lord. And it was a joy that would carry them through their life together.

They exchanged rings and vows, and then Pastor Calvano was introducing them as husband and wife and all their friends and family were clapping and they were walking back down the aisle.

In the lobby, Luke swept her into his arms. "Merry Christmas, Mrs. Foster," he murmured.

"So this goes in the good Christmas memories column?" she asked.

"The *best* Christmas memories," he corrected.

"And you admit you like Christmas now?"

"Oh yeah." He leaned closer as people started to file toward them. "I *love* Christmas. I thought you knew."

Madison laughed and stole a quick kiss before they were surrounded by people wishing them joy.

Thanks for reading CHRISTMAS OF JOY! Don't miss the full River Falls series, following the Calvano family as they find second chances, embrace new beginnings, and learn to rely on the Lord in all things. If you're wondering how Joseph and Ava fell in love, keep reading for a preview of their story, Pieces of Forever.

Also be sure to sign up for my newsletter, where we chat about life, faith, and of course books! You'll also get a free book, available exclusively to subscribers. Sign up at www.valeriembodden.com/freebook or by using the QR code below.

A preview of Pieces of Forever

Most days, Ava could keep the demons of the past at bay.

But today, every click of the shutter reminded her of what could have been.

"Okay." She lowered the camera from her face and studied the model-perfect teenage girl standing in front of the muslin backdrop. Ava had chosen a white background to give the photos an airy, ethereal quality. "Nice job, Emma. Now, can you touch your hand to your face?"

"Like this?" Emma lifted a fisted hand to her cheek as her friend Emily, whom Ava had already done a set of shots for, giggled from behind Ava.

"You look like that statue," Emily said. "You know, the one with the guy all hunched over?"

"The Thinker?" Ava smiled as both girls dissolved into giggles. She'd been fun and silly like this once too. Some days it felt like a long time ago. Other times, like now, those days bit close at her heels. "I was thinking more like this." She lifted her own hand to her face, wincing internally as her fingertips brushed the ridges of skin that puckered her left cheek. How did she forget sometimes that this was what her skin felt like now? What it would always feel like.

She forced herself to keep her fingers there until Emma mimicked the gesture.

"Perfect." She lifted the camera and started clicking again, calling for the girl to smile, then to be serious, then to make the goofiest face she could muster. The secret to great photos, she'd found, was capturing those moments when a subject was off guard, like in the seconds after Emma pulled her goofy face and then broke into a laugh that brought out her best smile of the day.

"Great." She set her camera on the table of gear behind her. "Why don't you girls go change into your next outfits, and I'll get things set up out here."

As the girls scampered off, giggling as wildly as ever, Ava switched from the white backdrop to a black one, then reset the light levels and repositioned her flashes.

All the while, she battled those demons. If life had gone the way she'd planned, she wouldn't be in River Falls, taking photos. She'd be in New York, on the other side of the lens. She'd be the one who was giggling and rushing off to change clothes and soaking up the spotlight.

But life didn't go the way you planned.

She shook off the heaviness that tried to hang on her. She had everything she needed—her own business, her aunt, and her dog. She'd decided a long time ago that it was more than enough.

It had to be.

Ava stepped back and surveyed the studio, tapping the smooth right side of her lips.

Something was missing here.

A chair, maybe. Or no—a ladder.

She was pretty sure she still had one among her props. She stepped around her equipment and bustled toward the back room, which served as both prop storage and a makeshift changing area, with two large changing booths off to the side.

When she reached the room, she stopped in the doorway, looking around. Things were strewn helter-skelter—flowers in a pile on one table, fabrics of different hues on another, shelves crowded with wooden blocks and blankets and one of those metal washtubs everyone wanted a picture of their baby in. Scattered among it all were chairs of various shapes and colors, trunks of every size imaginable, old lighting equipment, and a variety of tripods. It was getting to the point where Ava could barely walk through the space. Aunt Lori kept offering to come and help her sort through things, but Ava always declined. She knew that to Aunt Lori, sorting meant throwing away—she'd learned that in fifth grade when Aunt Lori had "sorted" a pile of Ava's paintings right into the garbage can. Anyway, she'd get around to cleaning up back here someday.

And until then, it was always an adventure.

Her eye fell on the ladder sticking out from behind a stack of large blank canvases she had yet to find a use for. Maybe she'd grab a couple of those while she was at it. They might look artistic leaning against the ladder.

"What do you think happened to her?" The voice carried from the dressing stalls, locking Ava in place. "A fire?" She couldn't tell if the speaker was Emma or Emily.

"I think so," the other girl's voice was quieter but still reached Ava. "My mom said she was supposed to be a model or something."

"Wow. You would never be able to tell."

Ava closed her eyes, allowing herself a slow count of five. She'd heard worse. And it wasn't like the girls were trying to hurt her. They thought she was up front.

And they were only being honest.

"Wouldn't you just want to die if that happened to you?"

"Emma!" Emily's voice scolded around a half-laugh.

"Sorry. But you know what I mean. She's never going to have a boyfriend or anything."

"I heard she used to date one of the Calvano brothers. In high school."

"Ooh. Which one? They're all so hot."

"Ew." Emily made a retching sound. "They're *old*, Emma."

"Not that old. The youngest was in my sister's class, and she's only twenty."

"Well, I can't remember which one she dated. But I guess he totally ghosted her after . . ."

Ava's swallow sliced her throat as she backed out of the room, letting the girls' voices fade.

"Joseph," she wanted to say. He was the Calvano brother she'd dated. But she pressed her lips together and silently moved back into the studio.

There, she forced herself to pick up her camera, to double-check the ISO and the aperture, to shoot a test picture and check the white balance.

Forced herself, when Emma and Emily returned in their new outfits, to smile and nod and take pictures that would highlight their unmarred beauty.

Forced herself, when they were done, to hold her head high and say goodbye as they draped themselves over the boys who had come to pick them up.

Forced herself, as she locked the studio door, to remember that she had chosen this. That she had been the one to do the ghosting, not him.

Not that it mattered. If she hadn't pushed him away, he would have run. And she wouldn't have blamed him.

Chapter 2

It was finally happening.

Joseph sat in his car, staring at the low brick building where he'd gotten his first job when he was fourteen. He'd had to beg Dr. Gallagher for weeks for that job. But finally the old vet had taken pity on him and let him help with cleaning kennels. From there, he'd worked his way up to checking in patients and then assisting the vet with minor procedures. When Joseph had graduated high school, Dr. Gallagher had promised that if Joseph studied to become a vet, he would sell him the practice one day. And now, after eight grueling years of school, River Falls Veterinary was his.

"Holy smokes," he whispered to himself. What if, after all this time, he didn't have what it took? What if he ran the practice Dr. Gallagher had spent forty years building right into the ground?

Something cold and wet pressed to his cheek, and he laughed, patting his Samoyed's soft white ears. The dog was just what he needed to keep himself grounded.

"You're right, Tasha. God's got this. What are we waiting for?"

He opened his car door, patting the roof. He'd been driving the thing for a decade, and he hadn't been sure it'd get him home from Cornell, but it had. Of course, with the loan he'd just signed to buy the practice, this old rust-bucket was going to have to get him through for a while longer.

Tasha zoomed past him, her nose instantly to the ground. Joseph wondered how many dogs had walked through the doors of this building over the years. He pulled out his keychain and grabbed the key that had been on it for less than an hour, taking a deep breath as he turned it in the lock.

This was it.

He pushed the door open and stepped over the threshold into the next chapter of his life.

Inside, everything was exactly the way Joseph remembered it, right down to the magazines in the racks and the paw-shaped treat bowl on the counter. Dr. Gallagher had even left the hideous paintings of cats in tuxedos.

"Maybe we can replace those," Joseph muttered to Tasha. And he knew exactly who he wanted to paint the replacement pictures. Assuming she would give him the time of day.

But for now, he had work to do. "All right," he said to the dog. "Where do we start?"

Four hours later, Joseph had completed an inventory, placed an order for supplies and medications, and surveyed his patient list for next week. Fortunately, Dr. Gallagher had let patients with upcoming appointments know about the transition—and the majority of them had agreed to continue using River Falls Veterinary with Joseph at the helm.

He thanked God again that he didn't have to start over from scratch.

And while he was talking to God . . . *You know how much I want things to work with Ava this time, Lord. Please make it possible. Or at least let her be willing to talk to me.*

"All right, Tasha. Should we call it a day? Go get us both some treats?" At the last word, the dog's upright ears perked.

Of course, since Joseph had just moved into his new house yesterday and hadn't had a chance to get food yet, any treats were going to have to come after a trip to the grocery store.

"Sorry, girl. I'm going to have to drop you off at home first. It's too hot to leave you in the car." After spending the past eight years in New York, it was going to take a while to readjust to the Tennessee heat.

Twenty minutes later, with Tasha safely dropped off at home, Joseph drove past the familiar storefronts that had lined Main Street since he was a boy: Daisy's Pie Shop, Henderson's Art Gallery, the Sweet Boutique, the Book Den. He crossed the bridge over the Serenity River, driving to the outskirts of town, where the grocery store was located. Sweating lightly after the short walk across the parking lot, he ducked gratefully into the air conditioned store.

He reached for a cart just as another hand landed on it.

A female hand, judging by the bright pink nail polish.

"Oh sorry." Joseph pulled his hand back and reached for another cart.

"Joseph Calvano?" The woman's voice was warm and sugary, slightly higher than most, with a taste of the South that he'd missed during his years in New York. It was a voice he would recognize anywhere.

"Madison Monroe." He turned toward her, holding out his hand, but she dove at him in a hug.

He hesitated a second, then lifted a reluctant arm to her back.

"Your daddy said you were coming home," Madison said as she pulled away, her eyes traveling to his shoes, then back up to his shoulders.

"It's nice to see you," Joseph mumbled. The last time he'd talked to Madison had been as he was running out of the prom he'd taken her to.

"You too. We should get together sometime. Catch up. You owe me a dance, you know."

"Yeah. Um—" He'd never had any desire to take Madison to the prom. He'd only asked her because he was upset that the girl he'd wanted to take—the only girl he'd ever wanted to do anything with—had pushed him away. "Sorry about that." He'd never before considered that it might have bothered Madison. She had so many guys falling at her feet, he figured she probably hadn't even noticed.

"I forgive you. On one condition." Madison pointed her perfectly manicured fingernail at his chest.

"What's that?"

"Dinner. Tomorrow night."

"Oh." Joseph's mind whirred. "I'm sorry, I can't. I'm actually, uh, actually . . ." He scratched his cheek, hoping she couldn't tell he was stalling. "I'm actually seeing someone."

Technically speaking, that wasn't one hundred percent true. But he would be seeing someone soon—as soon as he worked up the nerve to ask her. And assuming that she said yes. That counted, didn't it?

"I should have known." Madison studied his face a little too closely. "You always were too good a catch to stay single."

Joseph had no idea how to react to that. The best he could come up with was a strange sound at the back of his throat. He grabbed for an empty cart.

Madison spun her cart toward the produce section. "I'm sure I'll see you around."

Joseph blew out a long breath as she disappeared. He waited a few seconds, then entered the store, making sure to choose a different aisle than the one she'd headed for. Thankfully, he didn't run into her again as he did his shopping.

As he emerged from the store forty-five minutes later, he tried not to be disappointed that he hadn't seen the one woman he really wanted to see. The same one he'd wanted to take to the prom. It would have taken a pretty big coincidence for Ava to be at the store at the same time he was on his first day home. Not that Joseph doubted it could happen—he'd learned over the years that even the seemingly coincidental was in God's hands.

He whistled as he pushed his cart toward his car, letting his eyes rove to the deep green slopes of the Smoky Mountains that wrapped around the town, making River Falls feel cozy and protected and tucked away in its own corner of the world. He turned his head to the north, squinting, even though he knew her house was too far into the ridges to see from here.

"Watch out!"

Joseph yanked his cart to a stop at the shouted warning.

A dark-haired woman glared at him. His cart was only inches from hitting her.

"I'm so sorry." Joseph steered his cart out of the way as he apologized. "I was lost in thought. Wait. Lori?"

The woman's glare didn't ease. "Joseph."

"Hey." He cleared his throat. Wasn't this exactly the kind of coincidence he needed? "So, uh— How are things?"

"Good." The woman crossed her arms in front of her.

Okay. This was not going well. If Lori was this cold with him, what did that say about how her niece would feel to learn that Joseph was home?

"Glad to hear it." He waited for her to ask how things were with him—to give him an opening to say that he was back in town for good. But she remained silent.

Apparently, he was going to have to take things into his own hands. "I just moved back to town. Bought Dr. Gallagher's practice."

Lori gave a short nod.

"Anyway, uh—" Joseph pulled on the neck of his shirt. Had someone cranked up the thermostat on the sun? "How is Ava?"

There. He'd done it.

Lori's mouth tightened, and he resisted the urge to remind her that Ava was the one who had broken up with him.

"She's fine," Lori said finally.

"That's good." He'd been hoping for a little more information than that. But he wasn't sure he should come out and ask if Ava was seeing anyone.

"She has a photography studio."

"That's great—" He grinned at the thought. Ava had always been artistic. He bet she was a talented photographer. "I'd love to—"

"And she's getting married," Lori cut in.

"I— She's— Married?" Joseph gripped the handle of his cart. His world was tipping. "That's—" He choked on the word *great*. He wanted to be happy for Ava. He really did. "Tell her congratulations from me, would you? I, uh— Wow. I should . . ." He gestured vaguely toward his car.

He didn't wait on Lori's response before practically sprinting away from her.

He unloaded his groceries, then climbed into his car and just sat.

Ava was getting married? To someone who wasn't him? How could that be?

He'd been so sure that coming home to River Falls was more than a chance to start his veterinary practice—it was supposed to be a second chance with Ava. A chance to keep the promise he never should have broken—not even when she'd asked him to.

KEEP READING PIECES OF FOREVER

Also By Valerie M. Bodden

More River Falls Books

Pieces of Forever (Joseph & Ava)
Songs of Home (Lydia & Liam)
Memories of the Heart (Simeon & Abigail)
Whispers of Truth (Benjamin & Summer)
Promises of Mercy (Judah & Faith)
Hearts of Hope (Zeb & Victoria)

River Falls Christmas Romances

Christmas of Joy (Madison & Luke)

The Hope Springs Series

Not Until Forever (Sophie & Spencer)
Not Until This Moment (Jared & Peyton)
Not Until You (Nate & Violet)

Not Until Us (Dan & Jade)
Not Until Christmas Morning (Leah & Austin)
Not Until This Day (Tyler & Isabel)
Not Until Someday (Grace & Levi)
Not Until Now (Cam & Kayla)
Not Until Then (Bethany & James)
Not Until The End (Emma & Owen)

Love on Sanctuary Shores

Trusting His Promise (Beckett & Jo)

Want to know when my next book releases?

You can follow me on Amazon to be the first to know when my next book releases! Just visit amazon.com/author/valeriembodden and click the follow button.

Acknowledgements

"To him who is able to do immeasurably more than all we ask or imagine." What a God we have! I admit that I was kind of like Madison growing up—I wasn't sure what I imagined for my life. I always loved to write and hoped and dreamed and wished to become a writer. But I didn't *plan* to. Because that seemed impractical, unlikely, a dream too big for even God to fulfill (oh, I had so much to learn!). But through a series of events I can't even begin to explain, God made it possible for me to write the books of my heart. When I started on this journey, I had no idea where I was going. But God did! And he has wildly exceeded anything I could have imagined. An opportunity to share his Word and his love through my books—wow! A chance to meet readers from around the world—wow! Joy in what I do every day—wow! My first and greatest thanks is always to him. And I pray that more than anything, my books will always give him the glory and reflect the joy and hope and peace we have only in him.

Of course, this journey has not been a solo trip. I am so thankful for my husband Josh who pushed me for years to pursue writing before I finally got it through my thick head that he might be on to something. Thankfully, he never gave up on dreaming big for me. And I am grateful for our four children, who have always taken it for granted that Mom is a writer but who also celebrate every time I finish a book. As they grow up, I am so excited to see all the things that I can't even imagine that God has in store for them.

I am thankful to my parents, my sister, my in-laws, and my extended family for their support and love along this journey. It's a blessing to be surrounded by such a large and encouraging group. And to the friends I've met along the way. What a gift you all are!

And speaking of the friends who are with me on this journey, I am so grateful for the wonderful group of advance readers I've gathered around me. It feels sometimes like having my own personal joy-bringers, the way you all encourage and uplift and support me. Special thanks to Vickie, Rhondia, Sandy Golinger, Mary S., Diana A., Margaret N., Lincoln Clark, JJ Leonard, Michelle M., Teresa M., Connie Gandy, Mary T., Becky Collins, Carol Witzenburger, Chris Green, DS, Evelyn Foreman, Trudy Cordle, Jen Ellenson, Carol Brandon, Patty Bohuslav, Karen Jernigan, Ilona, Chinye, Jenny M., JS, Lisa Gallup, Carissa Anders, Laura Polian, Kathy Ann Meadows, Terri Camp, Judith Barillas, Sandy H., Jan Gilmour, Connie Gronholz, J. Fipp, Karen H., Lynn Sell, Ann Diener, Tonya C., Sharon W., Kellie P., Becky C., Karen Bonner, Jeanne Olynick, Mary K., Kris Vanica, Brenda Willoughby, Cheri Piershale, Barbara J. Miller, Vickie Escalante, Korkoi Boret, Bev V, Bonny D. Rambarran, and Seyi A.

And as always, thank you to *you* for joining me on this journey. Whether this is your first book with me or you've read every book that's come before, I am so glad to have you here. Thank you for inviting my words and my characters into your hearts. I pray this book has been a blessing to you. May the joy of the Lord be your strength, now and always!

About the Author

Valerie M. Bodden has three great loves: Jesus, her family, and books. And chocolate (okay, four great loves). She is living out her happily ever after with her high-school-sweetheart-turned-husband and their four children. Her life wouldn't make a terribly exciting book, as it has a happy beginning and middle, and someday when she goes to her heavenly home, it will have a happy end.

She was born and raised in Wisconsin but recently moved with her family to Texas, where they're all getting used to the warm weather (she doesn't miss the snow even a little bit, though the rest of the family does) and saying y'all instead of you guys.

Valerie writes emotion-filled Christian fiction that weaves real-life problems, real-life people, and real-life faith. Her characters may (okay, will) experience some heartache along the way, but she will always give them a happy ending.

Feel free to stop by www.valeriembodden.com to say hi. She loves visitors! And while you're there, you can sign up for your free story.

Made in the USA
Columbia, SC
04 June 2025

58939943R00112